1st EDITION

Perspectives on Diseases and Disorders

Depression

Jacqueline Langwith
Book Editor

Other books is this series:

AIDS
Alzheimer's Disease
Autism
Breast Cancer
Cancer
Cystic Fibrosis
Diabetes
Down Syndrome
Eating Disorders
Heart Disease
Leukemia
Obesity
Phobias
Sexually Transmitted Diseases

1st EDITION

Perspectives on Diseases and Disorders

Depression

Jacqueline Langwith
Book Editor

GALE
CENGAGE Learning™

Detroit • New York • San Francisco • New Haven, Conn • Waterville, Maine • London

Christine Nasso, *Publisher*
Elizabeth Des Chenes, *Managing Editor*

For more information, contact:
Greenhaven Press
27500 Drake Rd.
Farmington Hills, MI 48331-3535
Or you can visit our Internet site at gale.cengage.com

For product information and technology assistance, contact us at

Gale Customer Support, 1-800-877-4253
For permission to use material from this text or product, submit all requests online at
www.cengage.com/permissions

Further permissions questions can be emailed to permissionrequest@cengage.com

Articles in Greenhaven Press anthologies are often edited for length to meet page
requirements. In addition, original titles of these works are changed to clearly present
the main thesis and to explicitly indicate the author's opinion. Every effort is made to
ensure that Greenhaven Press accurately reflects the original intent of the authors.
Every effort has been made to trace the owners of copyrighted material.

Cover image copyright Anyka, 2008. Used under license from Shutterstock.com.

LIBRARY OF CONGRESS CATALOGING-IN-PUBLICATION DATA

Depression / Jacqueline Langwith, book editor.
    p. cm. — (Perspectives on diseases and disorders)
  Includes bibliographical references and index.
  ISBN 978-0-7377-4246-6 (hardcover)
 1. Depression, Mental—Popular works. I. Langwith, Jacqueline.
  RC537.D4263 2009
  616.85'27—dc22   2008026074

Printed in the United States of America
1 2 3 4 5 6 7 12 11 10 09 08

CONTENTS

CHAPTER 2   Controversies About Depression

INTRODUCTION

O
ne day during the school year, typically in October, students at thousands of high schools throughout the country watch a movie and take a test. The movie is not about World War II or how the government functions; it is about depression and suicide. One of the questions on the test asks, "Have you thought about killing yourself?" The movie and the test are part of a mental health screening program. Some people think mental health screening programs are needed to identify teens suffering from depression and other mental disorders, get them the help they need, and prevent suicides. Mental health screening advocates think schools provide an optimum place for testing to occur. However, school-based mental health screening raises a host of concerns for some people. Among their concerns are that mental health screening programs are unreliable and will lead to overmedication of children.

The idea of screening high school students for depression began in the late 1990s when a handful of high schools across the country decided to participate in National Depression Screening Day, an annual event held each October. National Depression Screening Day was started in 1991 by a nonprofit organization called Screening for Mental Health (SMH) to help people recognize the symptoms of depression and find treatment for themselves or a loved one. Many school administrators decided to participate in National Depression Screening Day because they were concerned about reports that an increasing number of teenagers were experiencing depression and suicidal thoughts.

In 2002 school-based depression screening got a big boost when President George W. Bush established the New Freedom Commission on Mental Health. Bush formed the commission in response to statistics showing that millions of Americans suffering with mental illness were going untreated. One of the key tasks of the commission was to increase awareness of mental health issues and get help to those who need it as early in their lives as

Speaking at the University of Mexico on April 29, 2002, President George W. Bush announces the formation of the New Freedom Commission on Mental Health. **(Keven Lamarque/ Reuters/ Landov)**

possible. After many months of research and meetings, the commission decided that school-based mental health screening was a good way to identify depressed teens and prevent youth suicides. Schools were encouraged to establish depression screening programs. According to the commission, "Schools are in a key position to identify mental health problems early and to provide a link to appropriate services. Every day more than 52 million students attend over 114,000 schools in the U.S. When combined with the six million adults working at those schools, almost one-fifth of the population passes through the Nation's schools on any given weekday."

Signs of Suicide (SOS) and TeenScreen are the two largest school-based depression screening programs in the United States. The SOS screening program was developed by SMH, the same organization that started National Depression Screening Day. According to SMH, since its inception more than twenty-five hundred schools, located in all fifty states, have implemented the SOS program. TeenScreen was developed by Columbia University. According to TeenScreen, that program has been implemented in more than 450 communities in forty-three states.

Those who favor school-based depression screening say that its main benefit is finding depressed teens who appear "okay" but who are suffering silently. According to materials distributed by TeenScreen, 60–80 percent of teens who suffer from depression go untreated, and tragically many of them end up taking their own lives. Statistics show that suicide is the third leading cause of death for fifteen- to-nineteen-year-olds. Leigh and Jonathan Manheim did not know their son Garth was suffering from depression when he committed suicide in 2001. According to the Manheims,

At the time of his [Garth's] death, we thought he was doing fairly well—pretty good grades, on the tennis team, daily workouts at the gym, had several good friends, and no signs of drug or alcohol use. We knew he was emotionally fragile, had low self esteem, and problems with mood swings, but what we didn't realize was how lethal these symptoms could be, didn't see how his problems added up to a very dangerous situation.

The Manheims are convinced that school-based depression screening would have saved their son's life. In 2003 the Manheims wrote a letter to their local school board supporting TeenScreen. "This excellent mental health screening will help parents to know if their child is experiencing serious mental health problems," they said.

Opponents of school-based depression screening are not convinced that it prevents suicide. They think the programs incorrectly identify kids as suicidal or label them as having one or more of any number of mental disorders. Vera Sharav, director of the Alliance for Human Research Protection (AHRP), says the TeenScreen program has a false-positive rate of 84 percent. According to clinical psychologist Lloyd Ross, "TeenScreen's extremely high false-positive rate makes the test virtually useless as a diagnostic instrument." Ross says the questions on the test are "loaded." They are designed to plant the seeds of mental illness criteria and make an adolescent feel that normal, everyday feelings and thoughts are abnormal. For example: "In the past year, has there been any time when you weren't interested or involved with anything? In the last year, has there been any situation when you had less energy than usual?" Most people would answer yes to these questions, says Ross. According to Joseph Glenmullen of Harvard Medical School, the questionnaires used to diagnose depression "may look scientific," but "when one examines the questions asked and the scales used, they are utterly subjective measures."

Some people think school-based screening programs are a front for pharmaceutical companies trying to sell expensive medications. According to AHRP, "Healthy children are being branded as mentally unstable and/or suicidal, serving as a means to increase the market for psychotropic drugs." AHRP and others believe that most people who are identified on screening tests as being at risk of suicide or having a mental disorder end up being treated with antidepressants, antipsychotics, or other drugs. If the person is a teenager, he or she represents a long-term customer of the pharmaceutical companies. AHRP and other organizations opposing school-based screening say that one only has to look at the funding sources of TeenScreen and SMH to see that drug makers have a vested interest in screening. They say that drug makers such as Eli Lilly, Pfizer, and others have given millions of dollars to school-based screening programs, because they know they stand to make billions in profits from the sale of their drugs. "Screening is a drugging dragnet," says Jim Gottstein, president of the Alaska-based Law Project for Psychiatric Rights.

The TeenScreen Program stresses that it does not make treatment recommendations. "Our goal is to provide parents with information about a possible problem and to link youth in need to qualified professionals who can perform a complete assessment." TeenScreen points to a survey completed during 2002–2004 that showed that less than 10 percent of teens identified on its screening test ended up receiving any type of medication. Most teens received some form of psychotherapy instead. TeenScreen also says that it does not receive money from pharmaceutical companies. It is funded by private foundations, individuals, and organizations committed to the early identification of mental illness in youth and the prevention of teen suicide. "The TeenScreen Program has never received support or funding from pharmaceutical companies for screening," it states.

Screening for depression and other mental health disorders at school is a controversial subject. In addition to the issues discussed above, some people believe that screening programs violate privacy rights and parental control, and they worry that once begun, school-based screening will end up as a mandated requirement. However, others hold firm to the belief that screening is essential to improving the mental health of America's children and teenagers. They believe it is irresponsible, unethical, and immoral not to identify and help students who are experiencing depression or other mental health problems.

Depression is a disease that has many faces. It can cause moodiness or irritability. It can be more lethal than cancer. It can be loud and identifiable, or it can be silent and unrecognizable. In *Perspectives on Diseases and Disorders: Depression*, the contributors provide information, opinions, and personal perspectives on the disease in the following chapters: Understanding Depression, Controversies About Depression, and Personal Stories.

CHAPTER 1

Understanding Depression

The Causes, Symptoms, and Treatments of Depression

Paula Anne Ford-Martin and Teresa G. Odle

The following excerpt provides general information about depression. The main types of depression include depressive disorder and dysthymic disorder. Major depressive disorder is an acute and intense episode of depression that is relatively short-lived. Dysthymic disorder, or chronic depression, is milder and lasts for a much longer time. The authors provide information on the causes and treatments of depression and how to recognize the symptoms of major depressive disorder and dysthymic disorder. Paula Anne Ford-Martin and Teresa G. Odle are nationally published medical writers.

D epression or depressive disorders (unipolar depression) are mental illnesses characterized by a profound and persistent feeling of sadness or despair and/or a loss of interest in things that once were pleasurable. Disturbance in sleep, appetite, and mental processes are a common accompaniment.

Photo on previous page. The main types of depression are major depressive disorder and dysthymic disorder. **(Bubbles Photolibrary/Alamy)**

SOURCE: Paula Anne Ford-Martin and Teresa G. Odle, *The Gale Encyclopedia of Medicine* 3rd ed., Gale, 2007. Reproduced by permission of Gale, a part of Cengage Learning.

Depression Is More than Occasional Sadness

Everyone experiences feelings of unhappiness and sadness occasionally. But when these depressed feelings start to dominate everyday life and cause physical and mental deterioration, they become what are known as depressive disorders. There are two main categories of depressive disorders: major depressive disorder and dysthymic disorder. Major depressive disorder is a moderate to severe episode of depression lasting two or more weeks. Individuals experiencing this major depressive episode may have trouble sleeping, lose interest in activities they once took pleasure in, experience a change in weight, have difficulty concentrating, feel worthless and hopeless, or have a preoccupation with death or suicide. In children, major depression may be characterized by irritability.

In 2006 The National Institute of Mental Health estimated that about 6.7% of American adults are affected by major depressive disorder, and about 1.5% are affected by dysthymic disorder in a given year. Major depressive disorder has a median age of onset of 32 years, and affects women more frequently than men. Dysthymic disorder has a median age of onset of 31 years. Both disorders may occur in any age group, from children to the elderly.

While major depressive episodes may be acute (intense but short-lived), dysthymic disorder is an ongoing, chronic depression that lasts two or more years (one or more years in children) and has an average duration of 16 years. The mild to moderate depression of dysthymic disorder may rise and fall in intensity, and those afflicted with the disorder may experience some periods of normal, non-depressed mood of up to two months in length. Its onset is gradual, and dysthymic patients may not be able to pinpoint exactly when they started feeling depressed. Individuals with dysthymic disorder may experience a change in sleeping and eating patterns, low self-esteem, fatigue, trouble concentrating, and feelings of hopelessness.

Adults with Depression, by State: 2004–2005

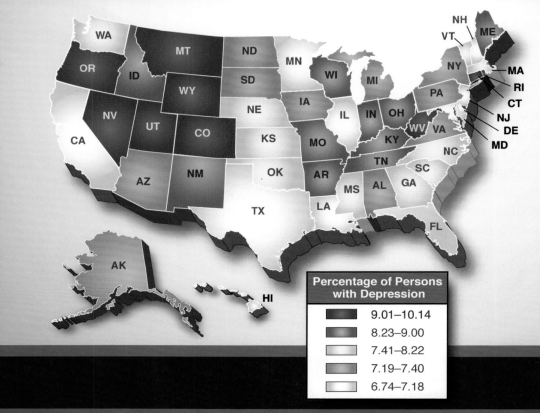

Percentage of Persons with Depression

- 9.01–10.14
- 8.23–9.00
- 7.41–8.22
- 7.19–7.40
- 6.74–7.18

Taken from: SAMHSA, Office of Applied Studies, National Survey on Drug Use and Health, 2004 and 2005.

Depression also can occur in bipolar disorder, an affective mental illness that causes radical emotional changes and mood swings, from manic highs to depressive lows. The majority of bipolar individuals experience alternating episodes of mania and depression.

Signs of Depression:

- Lack of interest or pleasure in daily activities
- Significant unintended weight loss or weight gain
- Difficulty sleeping or excessive sleeping
- Loss of energy
- Feelings of worthlessness or guilt

- Difficulty in making decisions
- Restlessness
- Recurrent thoughts of death

Causes and Symptoms of Depression

The causes behind depression are complex and not yet fully understood. While an imbalance of certain neurotransmitters—the chemicals in the brain that transmit messages between nerve cells—is believed to play a key role in depression, external factors such as upbringing and environment (more so in dysthymia than major depression) may be as important. For example, it is speculated that, if an individual is abused and neglected throughout childhood and adolescence, a pattern of low self-esteem and negative thinking may emerge. From that, a lifelong pattern of depression may follow. Many different factors have been linked to major depression, including chronic pain, severe obesity, and smoking (among teenagers).

Heredity seems to play a role in who develops depressive disorders. Individuals with major depression in their immediate family are up to three times more likely to have the disorder themselves. It would seem that biological and genetic factors may make certain individuals pre-disposed or prone to depressive disorders, but environmental circumstances often may trigger the disorder.

> **FAST FACT**
>
> Major depressive disorder causes more than two-thirds of all suicides.

External stressors and significant life changes, such as chronic medical problems, death of a loved one, divorce or estrangement, miscarriage, or loss of a job, also can result in a form of depression known as adjustment disorder. Although periods of adjustment disorder usually resolve themselves, occasionally they may evolve into a major depressive disorder.

Major Depression

Individuals experiencing a major depressive episode have a depressed mood and/or a diminished interest or pleasure in activities. Children experiencing a major depressive episode may appear or feel irritable rather than depressed. In addition, five or more of the following symptoms will occur on an almost daily basis for a period of at least two weeks:

- Significant change in weight
- Insomnia or hypersomnia (excessive sleep)
- Psychomotor agitation or retardation
- Fatigue or loss of energy
- Feelings of worthlessness or inappropriate guilt
- Diminished ability to think or to concentrate, or indecisiveness
- Recurrent thoughts of death or suicide and/or suicide attempts

Dysthymic Disorder

Dysthymia commonly occurs in tandem with other psychiatric and physical conditions. Up to 70% of dysthymic patients have both dysthymic disorder and major depressive disorder, known as double depression. Substance abuse, panic disorders, personality disorders, social phobias, and other psychiatric conditions also are found in many dysthymic patients. Dysthymia and medical conditions often co-occur. The connection between them is unclear, but it may be related to the way the medical condition and/or its pharmacological treatment affects neurotransmitters. Dysthymia is prevalent in patients with multiple sclerosis, AIDS, hypothyroidism, chronic fatigue syndrome, Parkinson's disease, diabetes, and post-cardiac transplantation. Dysthymic disorder can lengthen or complicate the recovery of patients with these and other medical conditions.

Along with an underlying feeling of depression, people with dysthymic disorder experience two or more of the following symptoms on an almost daily basis for a period of two or more years (many experience them for five or more years), or one year or more for children:

- under or overeating
- insomnia or hypersomnia
- low energy or fatigue
- low self-esteem
- poor concentration or trouble making decisions
- feelings of hopelessness

Diagnosing and Treating Depression

In addition to an interview, several clinical inventories or scales may be used to assess a patient's mental status and determine the presence of depressive symptoms. Among these tests are: the Hamilton Depression Scale (HAM-D), Child Depression Inventory (CDI), Geriatric Depression Scale (GDS), Beck Depression Inventory (BDI), and the Zung Self-Rating Scale for Depression. These tests may be administered in an outpatient or hospital setting by a general practitioner, social worker, psychiatrist, or psychologist.

Major depressive and dysthymic disorders are typically treated with a combination of antidepressants and psychosocial therapy. Psychosocial therapy focuses on the personal and interpersonal issues behind depression, while antidepressant medication is prescribed to provide more immediate relief for the symptoms of the disorder. When used together correctly, therapy and antidepressants are a powerful treatment plan for the depressed patient.

Antidepressants

Selective serotonin reuptake inhibitors (SSRIs) such as fluoxetine (Prozac) and sertraline (Zoloft) reduce depression

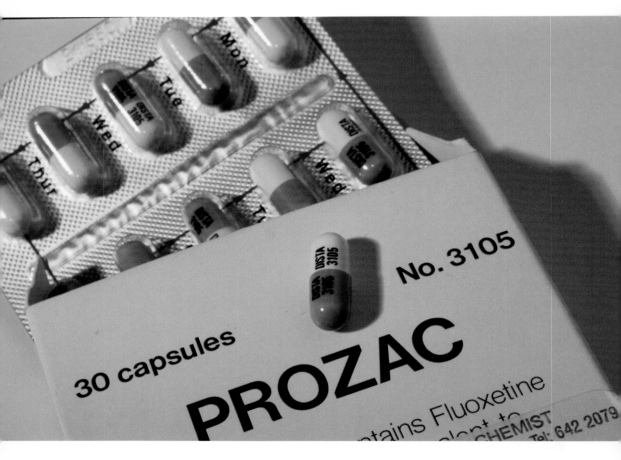

When used correctly, along with psychosocial therapy, antidepressant drugs such as Prozac can be a powerful treatment for depressed patients. (Dod Miller/ Alamy)

by increasing levels of serotonin, a neurotransmitter. Some clinicians prefer SSRIs for treatment of dysthymic disorder. Anxiety, diarrhea, drowsiness, headache, sweating, nausea, poor sexual functioning, and insomnia all are possible side effects of SSRIs. In early 2004, the U.S. Food and Drug Administration (FDA) issued warnings to physicians and parents about increased risk of suicide among children and adolescents taking SSRIs.

Tricyclic antidepressants (TCAs) are less expensive than SSRIs, but have more severe side effects, which may include persistent dry mouth, sedation, dizziness, and cardiac arrhythmias. Because of these side effects, caution is taken when prescribing TCAs to elderly patients.

TCAs include amitriptyline (Elavil), imipramine (Tofranil), and nortriptyline (Aventyl, Pamelor). A 10-day supply of TCAs can be lethal if ingested all at once, so these drugs may not be a preferred treatment option for patients at risk for suicide.

Monoamine oxidase inhibitors (MAOIs) such as tranylcypromine (Parnate) and phenelzine (Nardil) block the action of monoamine oxidase (MAO), an enzyme in the central nervous system. Patients taking MAOIs must cut foods high in tyramine (found in aged cheeses and meats) out of their diet to avoid potentially serious hypertensive side effects.

Heterocyclics include bupropion (Wellbutrin) and trazodone (Desyrel). Bupropion should not be prescribed to patients with a seizure disorder. Side effects of the drug may include agitation, anxiety, confusion, tremor, dry mouth, fast or irregular heartbeat, headache, low blood pressure, and insomnia. Because trazodone has a sedative effect, it is useful in treating depressed patients with insomnia. Other possible side effects of trazodone include dry mouth, gastrointestinal distress, dizziness, and headache.

Psychotherapy

Psychotherapy explores an individual's life to bring to light possible contributing causes of the present depression. During treatment, the therapist helps the patient to become self-aware of his or her thinking patterns and how they came to be. There are several different subtypes of psychotherapy, but all have the common goal of helping the patient develop healthy problem solving and coping skills.

Cognitive-behavioral therapy assumes that the patient's problematic thinking is causing the current depression and focuses on changing the depressed patient's thought patterns and perceptions. The therapist helps the patient identify negative or distorted thought patterns and the emotions and the behaviors that accompany them, and then retrains the depressed individual to recognize the thinking and react differently to it.

Electroshock Therapy

ECT, or electroconvulsive therapy, usually is employed after all psychosocial therapy and pharmaceutical treatment options have been explored. However, it is sometimes used early in treatment when severe depression is present and the patient refuses oral medication, or when the patient is becoming dehydrated, extremely suicidal, or psychotic.

The treatment consists of a series of electrical pulses that move into the brain through electrodes on the patient's head. ECT is given under general anesthesia and patients are administered a muscle relaxant to prevent convulsions. Although the exact mechanisms behind the success of ECT therapy are not known, it is believed that the electrical current modifies the electrochemical processes of the brain, consequently relieving depression. Headaches, muscle soreness, nausea, and confusion are possible side effects immediately following an ECT procedure. Memory loss, typically transient, also has been reported in ECT patients.

Alternative Treatments

St. John's wort (*Hypericum perforatum*) is used throughout Europe to treat depressive symptoms. Unlike traditional prescription antidepressants, this herbal antidepressant has few reported side effects. Despite uncertainty concerning its effectiveness, it is accepted by many practitioners of alternative medicine. Although St. John's wort appears to be a safe alternative to conventional antidepressants, care should be taken, as the herb can interfere with the actions of some pharmaceuticals, and because herbal supplements are not regulated by the FDA in the same way as conventional medications.

Homeopathic treatment also can be therapeutic in treating depression. Good nutrition, proper sleep, exercise, and full engagement in life are very important to a healthy mental state.

In several small studies, S-adenosyl-methionine (SAM, SAMe) was shown to be more effective than placebo and equally effective as tricyclic antidepressants in treating depression. The usual dosage is 200 mg to 400 mg twice daily. It may, however, cause some side effects, and an individual should discuss the possible risks and benefits with a doctor.

Proper Treatment Crucial

Untreated or improperly treated depression is the number one cause of suicide in the United States. Proper treatment relieves symptoms in 80–90% of depressed patients. After each major depressive episode, the risk of recurrence climbs significantly—50% after one episode, 70% after two episodes, and 90% after three episodes. For this reason, patients need to be aware of the symptoms of recurring depression and may require long-term maintenance treatment of antidepressants and/or therapy.

Research has found that depression may lead to other problems as well. Increased risk of heart disease has been linked to depression, particularly in postmenopausal women. And while chronic pain may cause depression, some studies indicate that depression may also cause chronic pain.

Patient education in the form of therapy or self-help groups is crucial for training patients with depressive disorders to recognize symptoms of depression and to take an active part in their treatment program. Extended maintenance treatment with antidepressants may be required in some patients to prevent relapse. Early intervention for children with depression is usually effective in arresting development of more severe problems.

There Are Many Kinds of Depression

Hara Estroff Marano

In the following article, Hara Estroff Marano asserts that depression is not a one-size-fits-all condition—it is a disease composed of many different subtypes. According to Marano, the boundaries between these subtypes are often unclear, with some overlapping of symptoms, and not every depression expert agrees on the classification system. However, the classification system represents distinct biological pathways of disorder that ultimately provides clues to the multiple ways depression can arise and express itself. The subtypes of depression can allow a doctor or a psychiatrist to know which course of treatment to take. Hara Estroff Marano is an author, journalist, and editor at large for *Psychology Today*, a magazine written from a clinical and an academic perspective.

D epression is not a one-size-fits-all condition. Mental health professionals have long recognized that patients tend to display reasonably

SOURCE: Hara Estroff Marano, "The Different Faces of Depression," *Psychology Today*, July–August, 2002. Copyright © 1991–2008 Sussex Publishers, L.L.C. Reproduced by permission.

distinct clusters of clinical symptoms, and they increasingly regard such clusters as subtypes of depression.

The boundaries between subtypes are often fuzzy, with some overlap of symptoms, and not every depression expert agrees on the classification system. But clinical research suggests that parsing depression into subtypes is useful in guiding treatment and in gauging the long-term outcome for patients.

At a symposium presented at a meeting of the American Psychiatric Association, doctors discussed five depression subtypes that together encompass the majority of depressed persons. These include:

- Atypical depression, which studies show accounts for 23% to 36% of all cases and is under-recognized.

- Anxious depression, which afflicts 40% of patients with major depressive disorder and poses many treatment challenges.

- Melancholic depression, a severe form of disorder that is most common among persons hospitalized for depression.

- Vascular depression, a newly recognized variety that reflects the existence of silent cardiovascular disease and is most common among persons over the age of 60.

- Psychotic depression, a severe form of disorder distinguished by mood-congruent delusions and accompanied by specific changes in brain tissue.

FAST FACT

According to Mental Health America, Utah had the highest rates of depression in 2004–2005. Among adults and adolescents in Utah, 10.14 percent experienced a depressive episode within the past year.

The distinctions first emerged several decades ago on the basis of variations in response to then-available treatments. But clinicians and researchers suggest that dissecting depression into subtypes may be even more valuable today. The subtypes may represent distinct biological pathways of disorder and may ultimately provide clues to the multiple ways depression can arise as well as express itself.

Atypical Depression

Atypical depression can manifest in both bipolar and unipolar depression, psychiatrist Jonathan W. Stewart, M.D., of Columbia University reported. Patients with this variety of disorder—about 10 million Americans— have what physicians label mood reactivity: they can be cheered up at least 50% in response to positive events in their life, albeit temporarily.

In contrast to patients with classical depression, those with atypical depression overeat regularly and binge of-

Those who suffer from atypical depression overeat regularly and binge often. (**Bubbles Photolibrary/Alamy**)

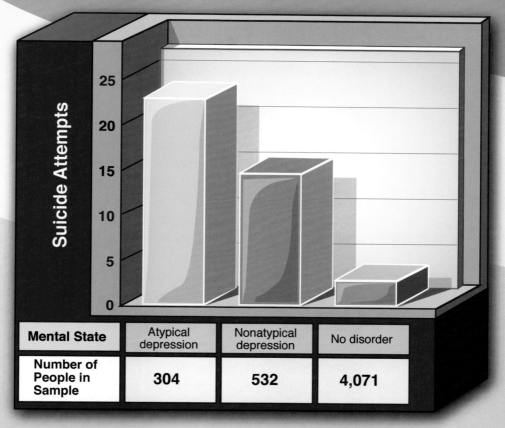

People with Atypical Depression More Likely to Attempt Suicide

Mental State	Atypical depression	Nonatypical depression	No disorder
Number of People in Sample	304	532	4,071

Taken from: Louis S. Matza et al., "Depression with Atypical Features in the National Comorbidity Survey," *Archives of General Psychiatry*, August 2003. http://archpsyc.ama-assn.org.

ten, gaining sometimes substantial amounts of weight. They also sleep a lot, and experience a leaden paralysis and overwhelming fatigue for much of the day, feeling as if they cannot even lift themselves out of a chair.

In addition to such physical manifestations, atypical depression is marked by a longstanding pattern of extreme sensitivity to perceived interpersonal rejection that affects functioning at work, in love, and with friends. With a trail of stormy relationships patients are either never married or divorced, and are unemployed or underemployed. Given their fear of rejection, many withdraw from relationships entirely and refuse to go on job interviews.

This variety of depression begins early—median age of onset is 17—and takes a chronic course. Depression afflicts many family members, and it tends to be of the same chronic type.

Perhaps the landmark feature of atypical depression is its responsiveness to one class of antidepressants, the MAO inhibitors. While they are no longer considered a first-line treatment because of their onerous side effects, they are regarded especially useful for people with atypical depression who fail to respond to other drugs. Cognitive therapy in conjunction with drug treatment is also effective and helps restore function.

A biology of atypical depression has not been delineated, as patients appear normal on most physiologic tests. But patterns of response to mixed-up images of faces suggests that parts of the brain that interpret emotion are not working normally.

Anxious Depression

Anxious depression covers the large gray area where symptoms of depression and anxiety co-exist or overlap. Patients typically have feelings of worthlessness and pessimism, excessive worrying and guilt, and are unable to enjoy things. The disorder is expressed physically in diminished appetite, poor sleep with frequent awakenings, and restlessness and psychomotor agitation.

In one study of 255 depressed outpatients that he conducted, psychiatrist Maurizio Fava, M.D., of Harvard reported at the symposium, 51% were found to have anxiety along with their depression. It's not clear whether the anxiety follows on the heels of feelings of worthlessness. But in 40% of the anxiously depressed, the anxiety disorder started first.

Among those whose anxiety takes the form of social phobia and generalized anxiety disorder, the anxiety tends to precede major depressive disorder. But in the case of panic disorder it usually follows the onset of the depressive disorder.

Patients are young—average age 20.6 versus 28.4 among those with major depression alone—significantly functionally impaired, and take more time to recover. They are less likely to respond to treatment and more likely to relapse, and experience less change in their depressive symptoms with treatment.

The disorder may have its origins early in life among children of a distinct temperament type who are frightened by novelty. Both the anxiety and depression may be the outcome of abnormaly high levels of hormones driving the body's stress response system.

Anxious depression typically poses a treatment dilemma for doctors. Many seek to use antidepressants that have sedating properties, although it's not clear that they need to, said Dr. Fava. Studies show that all of the antidepressants work equally well against this type of depression, although high doses may be needed. Still, in practice physicians tend to prescribe a combination of drugs for such patients, usually a tranquilizer along with an antidepressant.

Given their anxiety quotient, depressives of this type are unusually sensitive to bodily sensations. As a result, common drug side effects—such as gastrointestinal distress—are often cause for discontinuing treatment. Even when treatment continues, remission can be a long time coming. Cognitive therapy can be very helpful.

Melancholic Depression

Melancholic depression is often a synonym for severe depression, and it is far more common among those hospitalized for depression than among those in the community. Affected persons lack pleasure in almost all activities and do not react to pleasurable stimulation. They may experience extreme slowness of movement or agitation.

Their depression is regularly worse in the morning and is accompanied by lack of appetite and weight loss.

Melancholic depressives may also ruminate over the same thoughts and experiences, and feel excessive guilt. Their depression takes on a life of its own: the more episodes they have, the more autonomous such episodes seem, less likely to be set off by stressful events. And patients do not respond to psychotherapy, at least not before successful drug treatment, reported J. Craig Nelson, M.D., of Yale.

Studies he and others have conducted show that the most helpful drugs for this type of disorder are not the SSRIs but agents that block the reuptake of norepinephrine as well as of serotonin. "Some drugs," he said, referring to dual-action agents like venlafaxine and mirtazapine, "may treat more symptoms."

Psychotic Depression

Psychotic depression was once another term for severe depression, but the more refined the tools scientists apply to dissect the disorder, the more distinctive this variety appears, especially biologically. Not only is this type of depression severe, life-impairing and marked by suicide attempts, it is accompanied by delusions that reflect the depressed mood and guilt patients feel.

Biological tests show the patients have a distinct abnormality in the system that controls production of stress hormones, said Linda L. Carpenter, M.D., of Brown University. Imaging studies reveal significant brain atrophy. The decrease in brain tissue likely reflects the toxic effects of excess stress hormones, namely cortisol.

Despite the proliferation of antidepressant drugs, the best treatment for psychotic depression is electroshock therapy. But drugs now in development may offer some advantage. Dr. Carpenter specifically cites agents that interfere with cortisol by blocking receptors for it.

Scientists Are Making Progress in Understanding What Causes Depressive Disorders

Norbert R. Myslinski

In the following article, Norbert R. Myslinski discusses the causes of and treatments for depression. Myslinksi distinguishes between a temporary depressed mood that affects most of us occasionally and the different types of depression, such as major depression, dysthymia, and bipolar disorder. He further elaborates on the latest advancements in psychotherapy, pharmacotherapy, and electric and magnetic therapies, as well as what the future may hold for research and treatment of depressive disorders. Norbert R. Myslinski is associate professor of neuroscience at the University of Maryland.

B ased on advances in our understanding of the brain and its response to stress, promising new therapies for depressive disorders are on the horizon. . . .

Understanding Depression

Life is an adventure, with many ups and downs. At times, we accomplish our objectives and gain various benefits

SOURCE: Norbert R. Myslinski, "Offering Hope to the Emotionally Depressed," *World and I*, April 2004. Reproduced by permission.

and comforts; at other times, we stumble and fall, or the course of events puts us in difficult situations. Accordingly, our mood oscillates between joy and sorrow, elation and dejection.

Many people, however, find themselves stuck in a prolonged state of depression. Unable to shake off their gloomy feelings, they lose interest in activities they once enjoyed, and they no longer function normally. Moreover, their physical health declines, and their relationships with family and friends are adversely affected. They are suffering from clinical depression—a serious mood disorder, not a passing phase of feeling "blue."

Clinical depression can occur in several forms. The three main types are known as major depression (or unipolar depression), dysthymia, and bipolar disorder (or manic depression). Taken together, they appear to be the most common group of mental health problems in the world, affecting people of every race, culture, and ethnicity. While a small percentage of children are affected, the elderly are much more vulnerable.

FAST FACT

The largest national depression treatment study, known as the STAR*D study— Sequenced Treatment Alternatives to Relieve Depression—included 2,876 participants and was conducted from 2001 through 2006 at a cost of $35 million.

It has been estimated that more than 20 million people in the United States suffer from depressive mood disorders. The cost in terms of lost productivity and medical care runs into tens of billions of dollars per year. . . .

During the last 50 years or so, three main strategies have been employed for the treatment of depression. They are (1) psychotherapy, which relies on psychological methods; (2) pharmacotherapy, which involves the use of medications; and (3) electroconvulsive therapy, which shocks the patient's brain with electrical stimuli. These strategies are still used today, with a number of modifications introduced over the years. As our understanding of depres-

Alcoholics are nearly twice as likely to suffer major depression as others and often self-medicate with alcohol. (**Phototake Inc./ Alamy**)

sion and methods of treatment have advanced, promising new approaches are on the horizon.

Psychotherapy

Many psychotherapeutic approaches have been used in treating depression, but the most productive ones seem to be (a) interpersonal therapy, which helps the patient develop his social relationships, and (b) cognitive-behavioral therapy, which gets the individual to critically examine and test erroneous assumptions derived from the depressed condition. Both approaches reduce the risk of relapse, as long as the patient continues with the therapy.

In most cases, psychotherapy works best when it involves the patient's spouse and family. They therefore need to learn more about the illness and how they can offer emotional support and assist with interpersonal issues.

Researchers are currently looking into new applications for existing psychotherapeutic techniques. For instance, they are investigating problem-solving approaches that can be used by the primary care provider, and they are testing a modified form of behavior therapy (called dialectic behavior therapy) for depressed elderly with personality disorders. More research is needed to establish optimal conditions for using the new approaches.

It should be noted that not all individuals respond to psychotherapy, and only a minority achieve full remission. A combination of psychotherapy and antidepressant medication is more effective than either used alone.

Pharmacotherapy

Current pharmacotherapy is based on the monoamine hypothesis, which holds that depression is the result of depressed levels of certain substances—classified as monoamines—in the brain. The three main monoamines are serotonin, dopamine, and norepinephrine, which function as neurotransmitters (chemical messengers) that carry messages from one neuron (nerve cell) to the next.

Today's antidepressant drugs enhance the levels of monoamines in the brain (particularly in the synaptic gaps between neurons), by either preventing their degradation by enzymes or blocking their reabsorption into the neurons that released them. There are three categories of these drugs: (1) TCAs (tricyclic antidepressants), which include imipramine (Tofranil) and amitriptyline (Elavil); (2) MAOIs (monoamine oxidase inhibitors), such as phenelzine (Nardil) and isocarboxazid (Marplan); and (3) SSRIs (selective serotonin reuptake inhibitors), such as fluoxetine (Prozac), sertraline (Zoloft), and paroxetine (Paxil).

These medications have several limitations. It may take as long as six weeks of treatment before an initial therapeutic effect is felt, and longer for maximum relief. Moreover, the drugs relieve depression in less than 70 percent of patients who take them. After two months of treatment, only 35–45 percent of patients taking standard doses of the most common antidepressants return to premorbid levels of functioning.

The drugs also produce a number of side effects, some of which are serious. They should therefore be taken with caution and only as advised by a qualified physician. When taking MAOIs, the patient must follow a strict diet to avoid harmful effects.

In searching for better medications, researchers are now basing their work on the stress hypothesis, which states that depression is due to long-term stress, raising the level of stress hormones—such as cortisol—and causing our body's homeostatic mechanisms (which maintain equilibrium of various substances in the body) to malfunction.

Many types of stress enhance the secretion of cortcotropin-releasing factor (CRF) from the hypothalamus in the brain, setting off a cascade of events. CRF stimulates the secretion of corticotropin (adrenocorticotropic hormone, ACTH) from the pituitary gland, and ACTH in turn stimulates the release of cortisol from the adrenal glands.

Several lines of evidence suggest a connection between depression and elevated levels of CRF and cortisol. For example, when CRF has been directly administered into the brains of experimental animals, the animals have shown symptoms of depression, including difficulty in sleeping, changes of eating habits, and lack of interest in copulation.

Cortisol belongs to a group of steroids known as glucocorticoids. People suffering from rheumatoid arthritis are often treated with glucocorticoids, which have anti-inflammatory properties, but one possible side effect is the onset of depression.

In light of the stress hypothesis and the above observations, a number of research teams are looking for drugs that can inhibit or reverse the action of CRF or cortisol. For instance, the NIMH [National Institute of Mental Health] and several pharmaceutical companies are studying CRF antagonists—that is, substances that prevent CRF from exerting its effects. These drugs seem promising in the treatment of both depression and anxiety disorders.

Long-term elevations of cortisol levels in the blood can also inhibit the action of brain-derived neurotrophic factor (BDNF), a substance that is important in maintaining healthy cells and creating new ones. Inhibition of BDNF leads to the suppression of neurogenesis (neuron growth) and causes degeneration of parts of the brain, particularly the hippocampus and prefrontal cortex. Autopsy studies have shown that the hippocampus is 10–20 percent smaller in depressed individuals. This shrinkage can lead to difficulties in learning and remembering.

Some researchers are therefore looking for drugs that stimulate neurogenesis. Professor Rene Hen of Columbia University has shown that neurogenesis is necessary for traditional antidepressants to work. It now appears that a class of drugs known as PDE (phosphodiesterase) inhibitors, as well as BDNF and classical antidepressants, can alter not only the function of the brain but also its structure by stimulating the growth of new neurons.

Substance P, a neuropeptide known for its involvement in the sensation of pain, is another chemical released in response to stress. It is found in the prefrontal cortex, the hippocampus, and other regions of the brain associated with regulating emotion. While studying the substance P antagonist named MK-869, researchers at Merck discovered that it was effective against depression. Several companies are now working on substance P inhibitors, which may be the next class of medications marketed for depression.

In addition to these approaches, there is interest in the antidepressant effects of inhibiting glutamate—the brain's main excitatory neurotransmitter—or stimulating dopamine, a neurotransmitter for feelings of pleasure. Glutamate, however, is so ubiquitous that nonspecific inhibition would lead to serious side effects. A drug that specifically inhibits some glutamate receptors but not others is needed. One such drug under investigation is memantine.

In the case of dopamine, any drug that enhances its effects may have a high abuse potential. Most pharmaceutical companies are therefore reluctant to invest in such medications. Even so, NIMH is working on pramipexole, a drug of this type, which is currently used to treat Parkinson's disease.

Electric and Magnetic Therapies

Electroconvulsive therapy (ECT) involves a procedure in which electrodes are attached to the patient's head, and an electric current is passed briefly through his brain, inducing a seizure. Just before the treatment, the patient is given anesthetics and muscle relaxants to prevent his body from thrashing about violently. His brain, however, undergoes intense electrical disruption.

We still do not know how this treatment works or if it causes permanent damage. It is usually reserved for severely depressed patients who are not helped by drugs and those who are suicidal and need immediate help, until other forms of therapy can take effect.

In the early 1990s, an American Psychiatric Association task force concluded that 80–90 percent of those treated show improvement. The relief, however, lasts for only a few weeks or months. To extend the duration of relief, some clinicians treat their patients with ECT every

Younger Age Groups Less Likely to Receive Treatment for Depression

Percentages of past-year treatment for depression among persons aged eighteen or older with past-year major depression episode (MDE), by age group, 2005 and 2006.

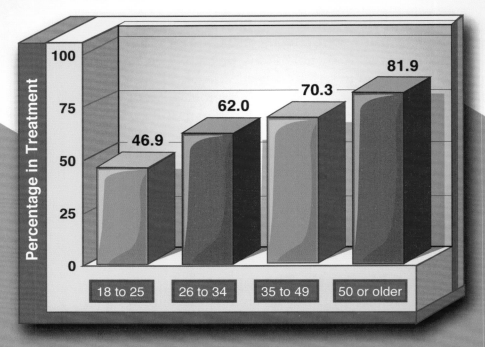

Taken from: "Treatment for Past Year Depression Among Adults," The National Survey on Drug Use and Health, Substance Abuse and Mental Health Services Administration, January 3, 2008. www.oas.samhsa.gov.

three to six months, but there is no good evidence of the safety of this approach.

Patient acceptance of ECT varies widely. Some greatly appreciate their improvement, but others hate it, especially when it is accompanied by memory loss. As many as 30–40 percent of patients report lasting memory loss. This can be very dehumanizing, considering that all our life experiences are stored as a collection of memories.

A safe, painless, noninvasive alternative now being investigated is transcranial magnetic stimulation (TMS). Clinical trials are currently underway in the United States, but this treatment is already available in Canada. It is one of the most promising nonpharmaceutical methods that can be used to switch areas of the brain on and off.

In the TMS procedure, a short pulse of electric current is passed through a wire coil (or pair of coils) placed over the patient's scalp. The flow of electricity through the coil generates a magnetic field that enters the brain. The field strength has been estimated to reach tens of thousands of times the strength of the earth's magnetic field, but each pulse is shorter than a millisecond. The magnetic field in turn induces small electric currents in the brain's neurons.

Unlike ECT, TMS does not require the patient to be anesthetized, and it does not result in memory loss. In addition, TMS can be focused on certain regions of the brain, while ECT cannot. One limitation of TMS is that the magnetic field can penetrate only a few centimeters into the brain's outer cortex. A single TMS session has virtually no side effects, except for a minor headache occasionally.

In the 1990s, psychiatrist Mark George was one of the first to study the treatment of depression with daily sessions of a modified form of TMS known as repetitive TMS (rTMS). In this procedure, the magnetic field is activated in several successive pulses. George found that repeated stimulation of the prefrontal cortex produced a significant (albeit small) antidepressant effect. Some patients who did not respond to other treatments benefited sufficiently from this procedure so they could be sent home from the hospital.

To date, the antidepressant effects of rTMS have been modest. In addition, rTMS can induce seizures, unless certain guidelines are followed. Research in this area continues to improve this technology.

A related treatment that creates beneficial seizures in depressed individuals is known as magnetic seizure therapy (MST). Described as a "supercharged" version of TMS, MST is performed on patients after they have been anesthetized. This method is being refined so that the patient does not suffer from memory loss.

Two additional methods, involving electrical stimulation of the brain, are currently being investigated for the treatment of depression. In one case, known as deep brain stimulation, a small electrode is implanted in the brain and connected to a pacemaker in the chest. The pacemaker sends high-frequency electrical impulses to the electrode, thereby activating that part of the brain. In the second method, named vagus nerve stimulation, a stimulator implanted in the chest is connected to an electrode attached to the left vagus nerve—a nerve that runs through the neck and connects parts of the body to the brain. In this case, the brain is stimulated indirectly via the vagus nerve.

Future Outlook

Clinical depression involves not only environmental factors, such as stress, but genetic factors as well. One would expect, for instance, the involvement of genes coding for such substances as the monoamines, CRF, cortisol, BDNF, and their receptors. It is therefore thought that gene therapy will be a future approach to controlling depression. A critical challenge will be to deliver appropriate genes to the intended neurons.

To date, no specific genes causing depression have been definitively identified, but numerous suggestions have been made. For example, some familial types of depression are thought to be related to a gene for a protein that transports serotonin across membranes. With a disorder as complex as depression, however, the risk of developing it seems associated with the products of many genes interacting with one another and with nongenetic factors.

Additional treatments that have been contemplated include the use of pacemakers or emotional gene chips implanted in patients' brains. Yet, until the new treatment modalities are perfected, most cases of depression will continue to be treated with established therapies.

However that may be, any treatment is effective only if it is used. Most people who have clinical depression are not treated. Almost half of those who are depressed do not ask for help, and only one person in five who need treatment ends up receiving it. The longer a depressed individual goes without treatment, the more resistant to treatment he becomes.

An immediate task is to educate the public to recognize serious depression in themselves and others, and to understand that it is a treatable medical disorder. Researchers, clinicians, and policymakers should be involved in finding ways to deliver effective therapies to those who need them, regardless of the patients' social or economic status. Unless a concerted effort is made to do so, our search for more effective treatments will carry little weight.

Deep Brain Stimulation Is a Promising New Treatment for Depression

Greg Mone

In the following article Greg Mone says that deep brain stimulation offers help to many patients whose depression does not respond to other treatments. Deep brain stimulation (DBS) is a technique similar to electroshock therapy, but milder. In DBS, electrodes deliver small electrical impulses to precise areas of the brain. Mone explains how DBS allows one depression patient to wake up every morning with hope and happiness. Mone is an associate editor at *Popular Science* magazine.

I n the middle of room #11 in the Cleveland Clinic's surgical center, Diane Hire lies on an operating table, the back half of her shaven head hidden behind a plastic curtain. Four pins, one driven into either side of her forehead, the other two in back, hold a titanium halo fast to her skull. An anesthesiologist, several nurses and her psychiatrist cluster around the bed.

SOURCE: Greg Mone, "Happiness Is a Warm Electrode," *Popular Science*, September 2007. Reproduced by permission.

Behind the curtain, neurosurgeon Ali R. Rezai surveys Hire's brain, white and snaked with thin red arteries, through a pair of small holes he's drilled in the top of her skull. Because so few pain receptors are located in the brain, only local anesthetic numbs Hire's head. She is awake during the procedure—or as awake as she can be. For the past 20 years, she has suffered from severe depression, a crippling strain of the disease that afflicts as many as four million people. Years of therapy, at least 10 different drugs and six courses of the whole-brain shock technique known as electroconvulsive therapy (ECT) all failed to bring Hire lasting relief.

Deep Brain Stimulation like a Pacemaker in the Brain

Her final hope is this operation, a radical form of neurosurgery called deep-brain stimulation, or DBS. Whereas ECT—a treatment that's been demonized in movies like *One Flew over the Cuckoo's Nest* but is still used on roughly 100,000 patients a year—floods the brain with electricity from the outside, this technique delivers a smaller dose of better-targeted current to an area of the brain believed to be a key regulator of mood. Wires thread beneath the skin from their place in the brain and plug into two battery-run stimulators implanted in the chest. About the size of an iPod nano, each stimulator constantly pumps out current, bathing a small region of brain tissue in electricity. If ECT is the equivalent of slapping defibrillators against a heart-attack victim's chest, deep-brain stimulation is the pacemaker that prevents the attack in the first place.

On the operating table, Hire closes her eyes. Rezai slowly inserts a wire as thin as a fishing line through the left hole in her skull, using the halo as a guide. His team has already mapped out his route using a precise 3-D reconstruction of Hire's brain compiled from 180 MRI scans. His target is a chunk of neurons associated with

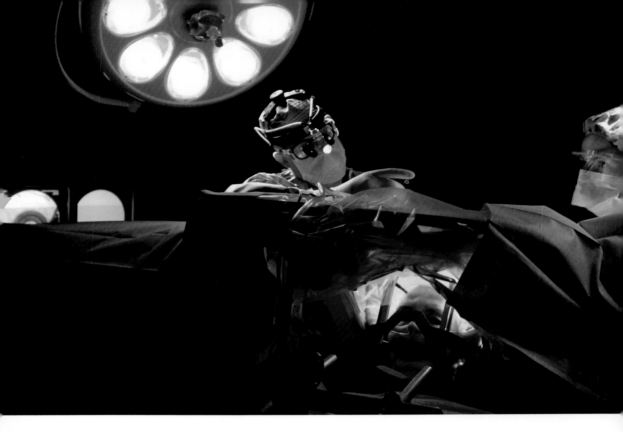

In deep brain stimulation small electrodes are surgically implanted in a patient's brain to deliver electrical impulses to help alleviate depression. (Michael Ventura/Alamy)

energy and mood. After the tip of the wire is in the right spot, he repeats the process on the other side. Within 90 minutes of the first cut, Hire has two electrodes lodged in the center of her brain. Now it's time to charge them up. On the other side of the curtain, Donald A. Malone, Jr., Hire's psychiatrist, tells her that everything's ready. Malone has a clear, soothing voice and a comforting, boyish face. He's the kind of person you'd want to talk to if someone was about to shock your brain.

At his signal, two volts of electricity, enough to power a wristwatch, course through the wires and radiate outward from the tip a few millimeters in every direction. Millions of neurons bask in the electricity, and the effect is fairly immediate. Hire feels warm at first, a bit flushed. And then it happens. The room looks brighter to her. The faces, the big, circular lights overhead, the ceiling—they all seem clearer. Malone asks her how she feels. "I'm really happy," she replies, clearly surprised. "I feel like I could get up and do all sorts of things." But even more telling than her words is the look on her face. For the first time in 20 years, with a halo bolted to her head and two freshly drilled holes in her skull, Hire smiles.

From Parkinson's to the Complexity of Depression

Deep-brain stimulation began as a treatment for movement disorders in the mid-1990s, and the surgery has been performed on more than 40,000 patients, most of them Parkinson's sufferers, since then. In those cases, the current normalizes activity in the basal ganglia and thalamus —which dictate motor control, among other things— and can calm their shaking hands and limbs.

But the clinical trial in which Hire is enrolled, along with 16 other patients, is among the first to tackle depression. Other major trials are under way at Emory University and the University of Toronto. Exact numbers are hard to ascertain, but it's estimated that fewer than 50 patients in North America are walking around with wires in their brain.

In some ways, severe depression is a far more challenging disease to treat than Parkinson's. It can manifest in dozens of different ways and arises from a variety of complex factors, some genetic and some environmental. For instance, scientists are just starting to identify a class of what they call vulnerability genes. In essence, they come in two forms: lucky and unlucky. "If you have one version, you are relatively resilient in the face of stress," says Brown University psychiatrist Ben Greenberg, who is collaborating with the Cleveland Clinic group. "But if you have another, the more severe the stress you have in your life, the more likely you are to develop depression."

Most depression therapies address the disease as a kind of communications problem in the brain. When all is healthy, a neuron receives a chemical message from a neighboring neuron and dispatches a corresponding electrical signal along a nerve fiber called an axon. Then, at the other end, the neuron pumps chemicals on to the next cells.

Drugs attempt to improve communication by altering chemical signals. Prozac, the popular antidepressant, blocks the action of a pump that sucks serotonin, a key mood-regulating chemical, out of the gaps between two neurons. This leaves more serotonin in those spaces, supposedly improving the flow of messages between neurons. But why (or whether) this makes people happy remains unclear. Antidepressants may generate billions of dollars in revenue for pharmaceutical companies, but recent studies suggest that pills work only 50 percent of the time—and they don't do much at all for the millions like Hire who are severely depressed.

Deep-brain stimulation takes another approach, targeting the electrical signals that facilitate the chemical communication. The exact mechanism affected is still undetermined, but Rezai suspects that DBS works on axons, the central conduits of each nerve cell. These protein-sheathed fibers act like miniature telecommunications cables, passing messages from one end of a cell to the other. Rezai thinks the added voltage may be increasing bandwidth in the axons, possibly allowing them to carry more information— and more of the right information. In the long run, he hopes, identifying damaged axons could help scientists develop new methods of diagnosing and treating depression.

Zapping Depression Away

But first Rezai must convince his colleagues that attacking depression with electrical current is a good idea. Patients like Hire, who don't respond to drugs, therapy or ECT, reveal how little modern science really understands about depression, which is one reason why DBS tends to raise thorny scientific and ethical questions. Most Parkinson's patients are in their 60s or older, but victims of depression might only be in their 20s. Will it be safe, wonders psychiatrist Neal Swerdlow of the University of California at San Diego, for them to have the hardware implanted for six or seven decades?

Then there's the fundamental problem of delivering happiness on demand. Hire's psychiatrist uses a hand-held device to tune the voltage and frequency of the stimulators implanted in her chest. Although some patients might wish to manipulate the device themselves, Malone says self-control is unlikely. There's a risk of cranking the

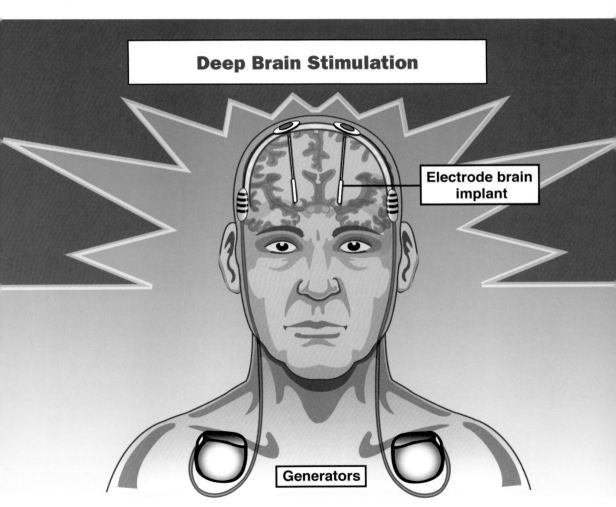

Deep Brain Stimulation

Electrode brain implant

Generators

volts too high, potentially causing brain damage. "This is not cosmetic neurology," he says. "This is about treating a fatal illness." Yet the trial-and-error process of banishing depression is still as much art as it is science.

To some, acting on this rudimentary understanding of DBS and its effects on the brain recalls the notorious history of operating on the brain to treat mental disorders. One psychiatrist, Jeffrey Schwartz of the University of California at Los Angeles, has compared the procedure to a lobotomy. Swerdlow is more hopeful. He thinks DBS, or some future derivation of it, truly could help patients and advance neuroscience along the way. His main concern is that the trials are happening too fast.

But Malone can't imagine going much slower. Time is dangerous in depression, with suicide—the eleventh leading cause of death in the U.S.—claiming more than 32,400 lives every year. For Hire, DBS isn't about unlocking the mysteries of the brain; it's about being able to get out of bed in the morning.

Treatment-Resistant Depression

Depression started controlling Hire's life in her early 30s. At 36, after 12 years of service in the Navy, she was medically discharged because of the disease. She went back to school and became a physical therapist. She worked and worked, trying to ignore her growing unease and inability to relate to family and friends, let alone strangers. She tried various drugs and met frequently with therapists. Yet the depression only grew stronger.

In 1999 she stopped working for good. She started semi-regular courses of ECT. The treatment failed to improve her mood and affected her short-term memory, a common side effect. Then, in 2005, Hire heard about

Malone's work with DBS and applied to be part of one of the first clinical trials of its use to treat depression. She and her therapist submitted a dictionary-thick stack of papers to Malone, documenting Hire's long battle with mental illness, but they got no reply.

By 2006, Hire rarely left her sofa, spent most days in sweatpants, and watched television from morning to night. It took her four weeks to work up the motivation to clean the house. That fall, she called her therapist and told her that she couldn't handle it anymore. "It was a really black, dismal existence," Hire recalls. "I just couldn't function."

As fate would have it, the very next day Malone called Hire's therapist with some excellent news: He wanted to meet Hire, if she was still interested, to begin the long process of determining whether she was a suitable candidate for the trial. The vetting could take months, but Hire didn't care. "I was at the end of my rope," she says.

Brain Imaging Shows Treatment Results

The day after her surgery, with her scalp sewn up but the wires still sticking out, Hire is moved to the Cleveland Clinic's main imaging center, where she's wheeled into a tightly packed room containing a functional magnetic-resonance-imaging (fMRI) machine. The device generates powerful magnetic fields to measure the metabolic activity in different areas of the brain in real time. It's shaped like a giant, nine-foot-wide doughnut and has a narrow bed inserted through the center hole. The imaging technician, John Cowan, helps Hire position her head inside the opening and outfits her with earphones and a microphone, while neurophysiologist Kenneth Baker squeezes behind the machine to attach the wires from her head to an external stimulator in another room.

From an adjacent room, Cowan, Malone and Baker watch Hire through a window and on a small video screen, talking to her frequently to keep her calm. For the next 48 minutes, while she tries to remain relaxed and perfectly still, Baker turns the voltage on and off as the machine scans her brain. For 30 seconds, she's happy. Then Baker shuts off the electrodes, Hire's smile fades, and the machine maps how her brain reacts. Another 30 seconds pass, and the happiness returns. Cowan later marvels at the effect of the stimulation on Hire and the other depression patients. "They're always laughing, and I'm wondering, how can you be laughing like this so soon after surgery?"

Regardless of how or even whether DBS is curing Hire's depression, the fMRI scans show that physiological changes in her brain accompany the emotional changes. The scientists can watch different brain areas—which they refer to as "nodes" or "hubs" in a larger circuit—become active, one after the other, in a repetitive pattern. "We're putting electrical impulses into a hub that connects large parts of the brain involved in your mood, your anxiety and your energy level," Rezai says. The more that scientists understand about how the diseased brain functions, he explains, the more they will know how to find the faulty wiring or circuits responsible for it, and from there they can design the therapies to fix it.

Impressive Results Hint at Future

The results of these limited tests of DBS are impressive so far. In 2005 the Toronto group found that four out of six patients showed significant improvements. In 2007, psychiatrist Thomas Schlaepfer's group at the University of Bonn in Germany announced that all three of his patients were benefiting from the surgery. And the Cleveland-Brown collaboration reports improvements in 70 percent of their patients, half of whom are in complete remission.

Medtronic, a company in Minneapolis that manufactures the hardware for DBS, is working with the Food and Drug Administration to plan the largest study yet of depression and DBS—a 100-patient trial in which the scientists may delay stimulation in half the patients for six months, switch it on in the other half, and compare the results. Emory is also planning to conduct a blind trial.

The Cleveland-Brown group is even starting to think about next-generation versions of the technology. Rezai, for instance, envisions implanted sensors that could detect abnormal activity in key brain circuits and deliver the necessary jolts to correct it. With the help of Cleveland Clinic biomedical engineer Charles Steiner, he's also developing versatile electrodes that send current in a specific direction. These would create a more targeted pulse, enabling the psychiatrist to further fine-tune the stimulation to suit the patient.

Happiness from a Machine

In Hire's case, though, the existing technology seems to be working just fine. When I meet with her six months after the surgery, she doesn't look like a person who spent 20 years trapped in a dark mental cave. She's energetic. She shakes my hand firmly and looks me straight in the eye—something she says she simply wouldn't have been able to do before. She laughs often (and my jokes aren't even really funny). She now walks 50 miles a week, talks to her family constantly, chats with strangers at the post office. And her smile is a regular, everyday thing, not a freakish, fleeting appearance in a crowded operating room.

The stimulation has been active since a month after the surgery, when, over the course of several visits, Malone adjusted the electricity, searching for and finding the optimal pulse. Yet Hire's depression hasn't been vanquished. The disease could still be triggered by life events—a death in the family, for example—which is why Malone and the other psychiatrists stay so heavily involved in each patient's life. But now if Hire starts feeling despairing or apathetic again, Malone can adjust the stimulation enough to ward off the darkness.

I ask Diane whether it bothers her to have her mental health regulated by a machine, and she shakes her head. For the most part, she says, she forgets there's a stimulator stuffed under her chest muscles and two wires snaking up her neck, into the depths of her brain. "I wake up every morning and feel like I control how the day's going to be and don't even think about, 'Oh, gosh, I hope it's still on,'" she says. "It feels like I have the power."

Millions of American Men Silently Suffer with Depression

Julie Scelfo, Karen Springen, and Mary Carmichael

In the following article Julie Scelfo, Karen Springen, and Mary Carmichael talk about the hidden epidemic of male depression. The authors provide numerous examples of men who suffered with depression for years but were unwilling or unable to seek help for fear of being stigmatized by those who believe that men are not supposed to "feel sad." Often male depression is masked by gambling, drinking, drug abuse, or anger, say the authors. The medical profession is responding and trying to help men recognize, acknowledge, and deal with their depression. Stigmas are fading, say the authors. Scelfo, Springen, and Carmichael are journalists who specialize in health and science issues. Their articles appear in *Newsweek* and the *New York Times*.

S
ix million American men [are] diagnosed with depression [each] year. But millions more suffer silently, unaware that their problem has a name or unwilling

to seek treatment. In a confessional culture in which Americans are increasingly obsessed with their health, it may seem cliched—men are from Mars, women from Venus, and all that—to say that men tend not to take care of themselves and are reluctant to own up to mental illness. But the facts suggest that, well, men tend not to take care of themselves and are reluctant to own up to mental illness. Although depression is emotionally crippling and has numerous medical implications—some of them deadly—many men fail to recognize the symptoms. Instead of talking about their feelings, men may mask them with alcohol, drug abuse, gambling, anger or by becoming workaholics. And even when they do realize they have a problem, men often view asking for help as an admission of weakness, a betrayal of their male identities.

Hidden Epidemic

The result is a hidden epidemic of despair that is destroying marriages, disrupting careers, filling jail cells, clogging emergency rooms and costing society billions of dollars in lost productivity and medical bills. It is also creating a cohort of children who carry the burden of their fathers' pain for the rest of their lives. The [actor] Gary Cooper model of manhood—what [TV character] Tony Soprano called "the strong, silent type" to his psychiatrist, Dr. Melfi—is so deeply embedded in our social psyche that some men would rather kill themselves than confront the fact that they feel despondent, inadequate or helpless. "Our definition of a successful man in this culture does not include being depressed, down or sad," says Michael Addis, chair of psychology at Clark University in Massachusetts. "In many ways it's the exact opposite. A successful man is always up, positive, in charge and in control of his emotions."

As awareness of the problem grows—among the public and medical professionals alike—the stigma surrounding male depression is beginning to lift. New tools for diagnosing the disease—which ranges from the chronic inability to feel good, to major depression, to bi-polar disorder—and new approaches to treating it, offer hope for millions. And as scientists gain insight into how depression occurs in the brain, their findings are spurring research into an array of new treatments including faster-acting, more-effective drugs that could benefit those who struggle with what Winston Churchill called his "black dog."

For decades, psychologists believed that men experienced depression at only a fraction of the rate of women. But this overly rosy view, doctors now recognize, was due to the fact that men were better at hiding their feelings. Depressed women often weep and talk about feeling bad; depressed men are more likely to get into bar fights, scream at their wives, have affairs or become enraged by small inconveniences like lousy service at a restaurant.

How Men and Women Deal with Depression

Taken from: HealthyPlace.com, www.healthyplace.com.

"Men's irritability is usually seen as a character flaw," says Harvard Medical School's William Pollack, "not as a sign of depression." In many cases, however, that's exactly what it is: depression.

Male Depression Typically Misdiagnosed

If modern psychologists were slow to understand how men's emotions affect their behaviors, it's only because their predecessors long ago decided that having a uterus was the main risk factor for mental illness. During the last two centuries, depression was largely viewed as a female problem, an outgrowth of hormonal fluctuations stemming from puberty, childbirth and menopause. Even the most skilled psychologists and psychiatrists missed their male patients' mood disorders, believing that depressed men, like depressed women, would talk openly about feeling blue. "I misdiagnosed male depression for years and years," says psychologist Archibald Hart, author of *Unmasking Male Depression.*

Some of the symptoms of depression are so severe, like gambling addiction or alcoholism, they are often mistaken for the problem. David Feherty, the affable CBS golf commentator and former golf pro, began drinking at such a young age it became part of his personality. "I drank a bottle of whisky in order to get ready to start drinking," he jokes. By his 40s, he routinely consumed two bottles of whisky a day, and was in such physical pain, he thought he suffered from "some kind of degenerative muscle disease." During that period, he maintained a jovial front, and kept up a steady stream of on-air wisecracks during golf tournaments. "It was a problem that just, I don't know, ate itself up and got bigger and bigger and then, one day, bang, I disappeared." When he finally learned in 2005 that he suffered from depression, he felt a combination of shock and relief. "That was the most stunning thing. I just thought I was a lousy husband

and miserable bastard and a drunk," says Feherty. . . . "A mental illness? Me? I had no idea."

The widespread failure to recognize depression in men has enormous medical and financial consequences. Depression has been linked to heart disease, heart attacks and strokes, problems that affect men at a higher rate and an earlier age than women. Men with depression and heart disease are two or three times more likely to die than men with heart disease who are not depressed. Lost productivity due to adult depression is estimated at $83 billion a year. Over the past 50 years, American men of all ages have killed themselves at four or more times the rate of women, depending on the specific age range.

Encouraging Men to Acknowledge and Confront Depression

A general practitioner is usually the first—and often, the only—medical professional a depressed man encounters. In 1990, when Mark Totten began sleeping a lot, refusing food and acting sullen, his sister, Julie, suggested he see a doctor, but never for a moment did she think it was life threatening. "I didn't know anything about depression back then," says Julie. In November of that year, Mark, 24, lay down on an Iowa train track and ended his life. Totten learned afterward that her brother had indeed visited his primary-care physician but complained only of stomachaches, headaches and just generally "not feeling so great," she says. The doctor didn't make the connection.

Confronted with a patient making vague medical complaints who is unwilling (or unable) to talk about his feelings, the hurried primary-care physician often finds it difficult if not impossible to assess a patient's emotional state. To help clear that hurdle, researchers developed a simple screening test for doctors to use: Over the last two weeks, have you been bothered by either of the following problems: (a) little interest or pleasure in doing things? or (b) feeling down, depressed or hopeless? If a patient responds "yes," seven more questions can be administered, which result in a 0 to 27 rating. Score in hand, many physicians feel more comfortable broaching the subject of depression, and men seem more willing to discuss it. "It's a way of making it more concrete," says Indiana University's Dr. Kurt Kroenke, who helped design the questionnaires. "Patients can see how severe their scores are, just like if you showed them blood-sugar or cholesterol levels."

Depression-screening tests are so effective at early detection and may prevent so many future problems (and expenses) that the U.S. Army is rolling out a new, enhanced screening program for soldiers returning from Iraq. College health-center Web sites nationwide provide the service to their students, and even the San Francisco Giants [Major League Baseball] organization offers these tests to its employees.

At Clark University in Massachusetts, where Sigmund Freud introduced his theories to America, researchers are developing new clinical strategies to encourage men to seek help. The Men's Coping Project, led by Michael Addis, recruits men for interviews and discussion groups that focus not on depression but on how they deal with "the stresses of living." At a recent staff meeting, the team reviewed the file of a middle-aged local man who described himself as stressed, angry and isolated, but vehemently denied that he was depressed. In a questionnaire, the man indicated that he preferred "to just suck it up" rather than dwell on his problems and that he believed part of being a man was "being in control." Researchers decided that rather than say "you have a problem" or "you need help," they would praise his self-reliance and emotional discipline, and suggest that meeting with a counselor might be the most effective way for him to "take charge of the situation." So far, Addis

FAST FACT

Male military veterans in the general U.S. population are twice as likely as their civilian peers to die by suicide, a large 2007 study showed.

and his team have met with 50 men, some of whom said they would seek counseling, and they plan to interview another 50 before the program concludes [in 2008]. . . .

Help Can Come from Different Places

Often the person who seeks treatment isn't the depressed man, but his fed-up wife. Terrence Real, author of *I Don't Want to Talk About It: Overcoming the Secret Legacy of Male Depression*, says most men in counseling are what he calls "wife-mandated referrals." When depression left Phil Aronson unable to get out of bed, feed himself or even pick up the phone, his wife, Emme, the well-known model, physically helped him into the shower, found

A depressed woman meets with her therapist. However, men, in general, are reluctant to discuss their depression.
(Janine Wiedel Photolibrary/Alamy)

doctors and therapists, and drove him to appointments, even escorting him inside. At one point, when Phil became suicidal, doctors told Emme it was her job to make sure he continued taking his medication and keep him safe from himself. "It was such an incredibly awesome, all-encompassing responsibility," says Emme, who became the sole caretaker of Toby, their daughter, then 2 years old. Even when the depression began to lift, her husband's moodiness took a toll on their marriage and Emme's career. "I had to be caretaker, I had to be a supportive wife, I had to leave my work. I was developing a new TV show and had to drop it." Today Phil is recovered, and Emme is thrilled to once again have a partner who makes her laugh, contributes to the relationship and helps parent Toby, now 5.

Success and wealth offer no protection from the ravages of depression. At 46, Philip Burguieres was running a Fortune 500 company, traveling constantly and meeting with shareholders, when, in the middle of a staff meeting on a Tuesday afternoon, he suddenly collapsed. Doctors diagnosed him with depression and encouraged him to leave his high-stress job. But after a short hospital stay, he was back in the game and by the following year was running Weatherford International, an energy-services company with $3 billion in revenues. The pressure became unbearable, and in 1996 he once again took a medical leave. "The second one was a grade-A, level-10, atomic-bomb depression," he says. In his darkest moments, he was certain the world would be better off without him, but even then, he felt enormous pressure to succeed. "I want out, but am stuck because I have never quit anything in my life," he wrote in a hospital diary. Strengthened by counseling and a friendship with a similarly depressed CEO [chief executive officer], Burguieres attained what he describes as a "full recovery" and stepped down as CEO. He found new work running a family investment company and as vice chairman of the NFL's [National

Football League's] Houston Texans, positions that permit him to delegate more responsibility and have more fun. He also found that helping other people was the best way for him to get better, and since 1998, he has been privately counseling the numerous depressed CEOs who seek him out. "You get outside yourself; you don't obsess on your own issues," he says.

Stigmas Are Fading

Fading social stigmas are already making it easier for young men to come forward. Recently, Zach Braff, filmmaker and star of TV's "Scrubs," told a reporter from *Parade* magazine that he thinks he suffers from "mild depression." At colleges and universities across the nation, health officials are putting mental-health care front and center. At UCLA [University of California at Los Angeles], the Student Psychological Services moved [in 2005] from a basement office to a bright building in the center of campus across from Pauley Pavilion. In January [2007], center director Elizabeth Gong-Guy walked through the waiting room and noticed that every person there was male. "It was amazing to me," she says. "I've been doing this for 18 years and that's not something you would have seen even three years ago."

Social attitudes toward depression are changing, thanks in part to men themselves. John Aberle is a sales and marketing consultant, retired Air Force security specialist, part-time radio talk-show host, devoted husband, active father and a 6-foot-4, 250-pound body-builder who twice faced a depression so deep, he cried on his knees. He readily tells other men it's their duty to get better. "There's no crime in having a disorder, whatever it is," says Aberle, 38. "The crime is not dealing with it. It's your responsibility to be at the top of your game." Taking care of yourself physically, mentally and emotionally—maybe that's the real definition of what it means to be a man.

Women Are More Likely than Men to Suffer Depression

National Institute of Mental Health

In the following excerpt the National Institute of Mental Health (NIMH) says that women are at greater risk of developing depression than men. Factors that uniquely impact women and increase their risk of depression include both biological and psychosocial factors. Biological factors are related to hormone levels during puberty, reproductive cycles, and childbearing. Psychosocial factors include childhood sexual abuse, sexual discrimination, lack of social supports, and poverty. About twice as many women as men are the victims of sexual abuse, a strong risk factor for depression later in life. NIMH researchers are investigating the underlying factors involved in female depression. The NIMH is the federal agency responsible for mental health research in the United States.

D epression is a pervasive and impairing illness that affects both women and men, but women experience depression at roughly twice the rate of men.

SOURCE: National Institute of Mental Health, "Depression: What Every Woman Should Know," National Institute of Mental Health, National Institutes of Health, U.S. Department of Health and Human Services, 2005 (rev).

Researchers continue to explore how special issues unique to women—biological, life cycle, and psychosocial—may be associated with women's higher rate of depression.

Women Are at Greater Risk for Depression than Men

Major depression and *dysthymia* affect twice as many women as men. This two-to-one ratio exists regardless of racial and ethnic background or economic status. The same ratio has been reported in ten other countries all over the world. Men and women have about the same rate of *bipolar disorder* (manic-depression), though its course in women typically has more depressive and fewer manic episodes. Also, a greater number of women have the rapid cycling form of bipolar disorder, which may be more resistant to standard treatments.

> **FAST FACT**
>
> It is estimated that 20 percent of women and 10 percent of men will have an episode of major depression at some point in their lives.

A variety of factors unique to women's lives are suspected to play a role in developing depression. Research is focused on understanding these, including: reproductive, hormonal, genetic or other biological factors; abuse and oppression; interpersonal factors; and certain psychological and personality characteristics. And yet, the specific causes of depression in women remain unclear; many women exposed to these factors do not develop depression. What is clear is that regardless of the contributing factors, depression is a highly treatable illness.

Investigators are focusing on the following areas in their study of depression in women:

The Issues of Adolescence

Before adolescence, there is little difference in the rate of depression in boys and girls. But between the ages of 11 and 13 there is a precipitous rise in depression rates for girls. By the age of 15, females are twice as likely to have experienced a major depressive episode as males. This comes at a time in adolescence when roles and expectations change dramatically. The stresses of adolescence include forming an identity, emerging sexuality, separating from parents, and making decisions for the first time, along with other physical, intellectual, and hormonal changes. These stresses are generally different for boys and girls, and may be associated more often with depression in females. Studies show that female high school students have significantly higher rates of depression, anxiety disorders, eating disorders, and adjustment disorders than male students, who have higher rates of disruptive behavior disorders.

Adulthood: Relationships and Work Roles

Stress in general can contribute to depression in persons biologically vulnerable to the illness. Some have theorized that higher incidence of depression in women is not due to greater vulnerability, but to the particular stresses that many women face. These stresses include major responsibilities at home and work, single parenthood, and caring for children and aging parents. How these factors may uniquely affect women is not yet fully understood.

For both women and men, rates of major depression are highest among the separated and divorced, and lowest among the married, while remaining always higher for women than for men. The quality of a marriage, however, may contribute significantly to depression. Lack of an intimate, confiding relationship, as well as overt marital disputes, have been shown to be related to depression in women. In fact, rates of depression were shown to be highest among unhappily married women.

Reproductive Events

Women's reproductive events include the menstrual cycle, pregnancy, the postpregnancy period, infertility,

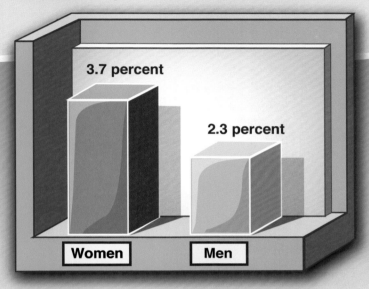

More American Women than Men Report Psychological Distress

Percentage of Americans who reported experiencing severe psychological distress, 2004–2005:

3.7 percent

2.3 percent

Women

Men

Taken from: National Center for Health Statistics, 2004–2005.

menopause, and sometimes, the decision not to have children. These events bring fluctuations in mood that for some women include depression. Researchers have confirmed that hormones have an effect on the brain chemistry that controls emotions and mood; a specific biological mechanism explaining hormonal involvement is not known, however.

Many women experience certain behavioral and physical changes associated with phases of their menstrual cycles. In some women, these changes are severe, occur regularly, and include depressed feelings, irritability, and other emotional and physical changes. Called *premenstrual syndrome* (PMS) or *premenstrual dysphoric disorder* (PMDD), the changes typically begin after ovulation and become gradually worse until menstruation starts. Scientists are exploring how the cyclical rise and fall of estrogen and other hormones may affect the brain chemistry that is associated with depressive illness.

Postpartum mood changes can range from transient "blues" immediately following childbirth to an episode of major depression to severe, incapacitating, psychotic depression. Studies suggest that women who experience major depression after childbirth very often have had prior depressive episodes even though they may not have been diagnosed and treated.

Pregnancy (if it is desired) seldom contributes to depression, and having an abortion does not appear to lead to a higher incidence of depression. Women with infertility problems may be subject to extreme anxiety or sadness, though it is unclear if this contributes to a higher rate of depressive illness. In addition, motherhood may be a time of heightened risk for depression because of the stress and demands it imposes.

Menopause, in general, is not associated with an increased risk of depression. In fact, while once considered a unique disorder, research has shown that depressive illness at menopause is no different than at other ages. The women more vulnerable to change-of-life depression are those with a history of past depressive episodes.

Specific Cultural Considerations

As for depression in general, the prevalence rate of depression in African American and Hispanic women remains about twice that of men. There is some indication, however, that major depression and dysthymia may be diagnosed less frequently in African American and slightly more frequently in Hispanic than in Caucasian women. Prevalence information for other racial and ethnic groups is not definitive.

Possible differences in symptom presentation may affect the way depression is recognized and diagnosed among minorities. For example, African Americans are more likely

to report somatic symptoms, such as appetite change and body aches and pains. In addition, people from various cultural backgrounds may view depressive symptoms in different ways. Such factors should be considered when working with women from special populations.

The prevalence of depression among African American and Hispanic women is nearly twice that of men. (**Bubbles Photolibrary/Alamy**)

Victimization

Studies show that women molested as children are more likely to have clinical depression at some time in their lives than those with no such history. In addition, several studies show a higher incidence of depression among women who have been raped as adolescents or adults. Since far more women than men were sexually abused as children, these findings are relevant. Women who experience other commonly occurring forms of abuse, such as physical abuse and sexual harassment on the job, also may experience higher rates of depression. Abuse may lead to depression by fostering low self-esteem, a sense of helplessness, self-blame, and social isolation. There may be biological and environmental risk factors for depression resulting from growing up in a dysfunctional family. At present, more research is needed to understand whether victimization is connected specifically to depression.

Poverty

Women and children represent seventy-five percent of the U.S. population considered poor. Low economic status brings with it many stresses, including isolation, uncertainty, frequent negative events, and poor access to helpful resources. Sadness and low morale are more common among persons with low incomes and those lacking social supports. But research has not yet established whether depressive illnesses are more prevalent among those facing environmental stressors such as these.

Depression in Later Adulthood

At one time, it was commonly thought that women were particularly vulnerable to depression when their children left home and they were confronted with "empty nest syndrome" and experienced a profound loss of purpose and identity. However, studies show no increase in depressive illness among women at this stage of life.

As with younger age groups, more elderly women than men suffer from depressive illness. Similarly, for all age groups, being unmarried (which includes widowhood) is also a risk factor for depression. Most important, depression should not be dismissed as a normal consequence of the physical, social, and economic problems of later life.

In fact, studies show that most older people feel satisfied with their lives.

About 800,000 persons are widowed each year. Most of them are older, female, and experience varying degrees of depressive symptomatology. Most do not need formal treatment, but those who are moderately or severely sad appear to benefit from self-help groups or various psychosocial treatments. However, a third of widows/widowers do meet criteria for a major depressive episode in the first month after the death, and half of these remain clinically depressed 1 year later. These depressions respond to standard antidepressant treatments, although research on when to start treatment or how medications should be combined with psychosocial treatments is still in its early stages.

CHAPTER 2

Controversies About Depression

Depression Is a Disease

Peter D. Kramer

In the following viewpoint Peter D. Kramer contends that depression is a devastating disease and that society should do everything it can to eradicate it. Kramer says depression has gotten short shrift as a disease because many people consider it a personality characteristic as opposed to a medical condition. Kramer is a professor of clinical psychiatry at Brown University and the author of *Listening to Prozac* and *Against Depression*.

It is true that among the major mental disorders, depression can have a deceptive lightness, especially in the early stages. Depending on the prevailing symptoms, the depressive may be able to laugh, support others, act responsibly. Depressed patients participate actively, even compulsively, in their own treatment. And depression, especially a first episode in a young adult, is likely to respond to almost any intervention: psychotherapy,

Photo on facing page. Controversy over whether depression is a disease has split the medical community. (Bubbles Photolibrary/Alamy)

SOURCE: Peter D. Kramer, *Against Depression.* New York: Viking Adult, 2005. Used by permission of Penguin Group (USA) Inc.

medication, the passage of time. In my medical school days, if an inpatient psychiatry ward had spun out of control, a cagey chief would hold off on admissions until a good-prognosis depressive was referred. The hope was that the new arrival's recovery would restore morale, for staff and patients alike.

But the depression I dealt with in my practice had settled in to stay. The unrelenting darkness was a function of the length of my tenure here. I have seen patients in Providence, Rhode Island, for over twenty years. In a small practice, failure accumulates. As I wrote more,

The ancient Greek physician Hippocrates put forth the theory that melancholia was a disease brought on by what he called "black bile." (Phototake Inc./Almay)

I let my clinical hours dwindle. The result was that patients who were not yet better filled many slots, along with those returning to treatment. And the popularity of *Listening to Prozac* meant that the loudest knocks on the office door were from families with a depressed member who had faltered elsewhere. Circumstance made me a specialist in unresponsive mood disorder. I worked amid chronic despair.

Many psychiatric practices have this quality as they mature. Light depression is depression in young adults; those patients were the ones ward chiefs favored. Suicide is always a risk; we worry over it and guard against it. Still, most patients in their twenties and early thirties do well. Often, a trigger for the acute episode is apparent, so there is something to discuss—the "precipitating event" and its relationship to prior disappointments. Psychotherapy plays a central role in treatment. The doctor feels of use. But as the patient ages, bouts of depression recur with greater frequency. Later episodes can appear spontaneously, without apparent reason. They last longer, respond more poorly to any intervention, remit (when they do) more briefly. Certain functions may remain continuously impaired—concentration, confidence, the sense of self-worth.

> **FAST FACT**
>
> According to the World Health Organization, depression affects about 121 million people worldwide.

Even with first episodes, there will be patients who respond poorly or incompletely. These hard-to-treat depressives linger in a practice. I will refer them for outside opinions. I will consider new and experimental interventions. Often, nothing works—or else, relapse follows hard upon recovery. These patients struggle. I knew them when—or just after, when life's promise was still evident.

For the psychiatrist, then, depression becomes an intimate. It is poor company. Depression destroys families. It ruins careers. It ages patients prematurely. It attacks their memories and their general health. For us—for me—the truth that depression is a disease is unqualified. Depression is debilitating, progressive and relentless in its downhill course, as tough and worthy an opponent as any a doctor might choose to combat.

In an important respect, my clinical practice stood at a distance from the testimony of the memoirs: I had never treated a seriously afflicted patient who, on recovery, said anything favorable about depression. Yes, in the grip of mood disorder, a patient may allude to a sense of superiority. The resilient are missing something; they do not get it. This belief brings comfort in a time of suffering. But the idealization rarely outlasts the depression. When she feels better, the patient will question her own prior thought process. What was this about? She mistook illness for insight. She had been, quite literally, making a virtue of necessity. In retrospect, depression has no saving grace.

Depression Is a Medical, Not a Moral Issue

Outside the consulting room, the tendency to attach value to depression is common enough. Depression can appear to embody an aesthetic or even moral stance. There is a left-wing viewpoint, in which depression represents moral distance from the culture, asthenic [weak] self-abnegation [self-denial], minimalism in contrast to mercantilism. There is a right-wing perspective on depression as well—the notion that one should "tough out" the suffering, without resort to "easy" remedies like psychotherapeutic support or medication. From either angle, left or right, there is a virtue in experiencing illness rather than seeking prompt and thorough treatment. At least, it seemed to me that I heard, in passing, claims of these sorts, claims that would sound peculiar in relation to any other disease.

They outraged me. I discovered in myself a protectiveness toward the depressed, a wish for clarity on their

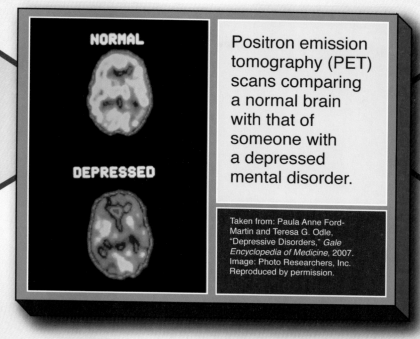

NORMAL

DEPRESSED

Positron emission tomography (PET) scans comparing a normal brain with that of someone with a depressed mental disorder.

Taken from: Paula Anne Ford-Martin and Teresa G. Odle, "Depressive Disorders," *Gale Encyclopedia of Medicine*, 2007. Image: Photo Researchers, Inc. Reproduced by permission.

behalf. I would have said that I had intended, on setting up my office, to conduct a broad psychiatric practice, extending to anxiety disorders, attention deficits, minor mental retardation, schizophrenia, marital discord, you name it. But if psychotherapy teaches anything, it is that, more than we are at first inclined to acknowledge, we are responsible for our circumstances. Chance plays a part, but we collaborate.

Depression Is Not a Disease

Bruce E. Levine

In the following viewpoint Bruce E. Levine asserts that depression is not a disease. Levine says the biochemical evidence for labeling depression a disease is lacking. Levine compares depression to alcohol, food, and television—strategies people use to shut down pain. Society would be better served, says Levine, if we called depression what it is—a reaction to pain. Levine is a clinical psychologist and the author of Surviving America's Depression Epidemic.

I f forced to choose between labeling immobilizing depression as either a character weakness or a disease, it's understandable that disease would be the preference. But there is a third choice, one that normalizes depression and which—for people such as myself—feels more respectful and better reduces suffering.

I regularly do battle with right-wing talk show hosts who mock depression sufferers as crybabies. Fundamen-

SOURCE: Bruce E. Levine, "Why I Don't 'Disease' Depression," *The Huffington Post*, November 27, 2007. Reproduced by permission.

talist pull-yourself-up-by-your-bootstrap yappers are often heartless and uninformed, and I tell them just that. However, fundamentalist depression diseases also need to be confronted.

"I have written a polemic, an insistent argument for the proposition that depression is a disease," is how psychiatrist Peter Kramer describes his [2005 book] *Against Depression.* . . . Kramer argues that depression must be a disease because of how devastating it is. He is certainly correct that depression can result not only in suicide but can ruin careers, destroy families, and stress the body so as to jeopardize physical health. However, such nondiseases as war and poverty also have a devastating impact; and there is a long list of noncontroversial illnesses, including the common cold, that do not have a devastating impact.

Calling Depression a Disease Based on Shaky Arguments

Kramer's other disease arguments are just as shaky. According to Kramer, biological markers—the sine qua non [absolute essence] of disease—for depression have been discovered. He tells us that brain scanning techniques focusing on the size of the hippocampus and amygdala can differentiate the depressed from the nondepressed. However, five months after *Against Depression* was published . . . the *New York Times* concluded: "After almost 30 years, researchers have not developed any standardized tool for diagnosing or treating psychiatric disorders based on imaging studies."

Kramer also proclaims, "Deplete serotonin, and depression is unmasked." But researchers have depleted serotonin, and it did not cause depression in nondepressed subjects nor did it worsen the depressive symptoms of those already depressed. By 1998 *The American Medical Association Essential Guide to Depression* had reported that there is no clear link between levels of serotonin and

Recent studies have revealed that serotonin, shown here as a molecular model, has no real link to depression. (Phototake Inc./Almay)

depression, "as some depressed people have too much serotonin."

Finally, Kramer tells us about the defective genes of depressives, "By the mid-1990s, scientists had identified genes that might lead to both conditions, neuroticism and depression." Kramer leans heavily on behavioral geneticist Kenneth Kendler; however, two months after the publication of *Against Depression*, Kendler reviewed the evidence for "gene action in psychiatric disorders" in the [July 2005] *American Journal of Psychiatry* . . . , where he concluded: "Although we may wish it to be true, we do not have and are not likely to ever discover 'genes for' psychiatric illness."

While symptoms of depression can be caused by a variety of medical conditions (for example, anemia and hypothyroidism), such medical conditions, according to the American Psychiatric Association, actually rule out the psychiatric disease of "depression." What psychiatrists call depression has not in fact been linked to any biochemical markers.

Depression Is a Crutch to Alleviate Pain

Depression is neither a character defect nor biochemical defect but rather a strategy to shut down overwhelming pain. Used in excess, it can lead to immobilization and greater pain.

Depression is by no means the only strategy people use to shut down overwhelming pain. People use alcohol, marijuana, television, food, gambling, and worse. A depressed Sigmund Freud, pained by failure, used cocaine, then turned his friends on to it, but ultimately discovered its adverse effects and rejected it. Joseph Goebbels [a prominent member of the German Nazi Party and close associate of Adolf Hitler], even more pained by failure than Freud, shut down his pain by embracing fascism; but, unlike Freud, Goebbels couldn't have cared less about the adverse effects of his strategy.

Labeling Depression a Disease Does Harm

Labeling depression as a disease gives some people relief, but such labeling creates grief for others. I have met many people who have been failed by antidepressants and electroshock. They talk about the adverse physiological effects of their treatments, but they also talk about something else. By becoming compliant patients to a medical authority, they describe losing control over their lives. Depression is an experience of helplessness and hopelessness and,

FAST FACT

Up to 25 percent of people may be misdiagnosed as having depression when they may only be reacting to normal stressful events, such as a divorce or job loss, according to a 2007 study published in the *Archives of General Psychiatry*.

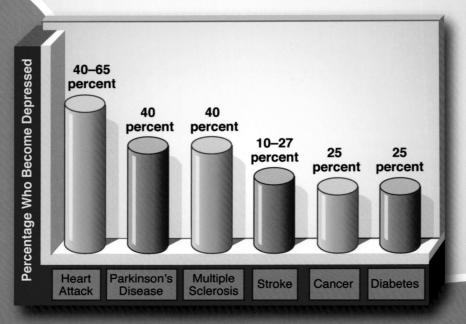

Chronic Illnesses Associated with Depression

Percentage Who Become Depressed

Heart Attack	Parkinson's Disease	Multiple Sclerosis	Stroke	Cancer	Diabetes
40–65 percent	40 percent	40 percent	10–27 percent	25 percent	25 percent

Taken from: "Depression Guide," WebMD, December 1, 2006. www.webmd.com.

for these people, accepting depression as a disease makes them feel even more helpless and hopeless.

Instead of labeling depression as weakness or illness, we might better decrease depression by understanding it as a normal, albeit painful, human reaction. When we label a part of ourselves as either "weak" or "sick," we alienate ourselves from a part of who we are, and this can create even more pain. In contrast, when we accept the whole of our humanity, we are more likely to be freed up to resolve and heal the source of our pains.

Antidepressants May Be Underprescribed

Jonathan Haidt

In the following viewpoint, an excerpt from the book *The Happiness Hypothesis* by Jonathan Haidt, the author challenges the notion that Prozac and other antidepressants are overprescribed. Haidt explains how Prozac and other "selective serotonin reuptake inhibitors" work to restore proper mental function. Haidt says that many people are uneasy with the fact that Prozac can so easily change people's personalities. But he sees no harm in using Prozac or other antidepressants to help the "worried well" feel better. Haidt thinks that antidepressants as well as other depression treatments should be made readily available so that everyone can benefit from them. Jonathan Haidt is an associate professor of psychology at the University of Virginia.

Marcel Proust wrote that "the only true voyage . . . would be not to visit strange lands but to possess other eyes." In the summer of 1996,

SOURCE: Jonathan Haidt, *The Happiness Hypothesis*. Cambridge, MA: Basic Books, 2006. Copyright © 2006 by Jonathan Haidt. Reprinted by permission of Basic Books, a member of Perseus Books, L.L.C.

I tried on a pair of new eyes when I took Paxil, a cousin of Prozac, for eight weeks. For the first few weeks I had only side effects: some nausea, difficulty sleeping through the night, and a variety of physical sensations that I did not know my body could produce, including a feeling I can describe only by saying that my brain felt dry. But then one day in week five, the world changed color. I woke up one morning and no longer felt anxious about the heavy work load and uncertain prospects of an untenured professor. It was like magic. A set of changes I had wanted to make in myself for years—loosening up, lightening up, accepting my mistakes without dwelling on them—happened overnight. However, Paxil had one devastating side effect for me: It made it hard for me to recall facts and names, even those I knew well. I would greet my students and colleagues, reach for a name to put after "Hi," and be left with "Hi . . . there." I decided that as a professor I needed my memory more than I needed peace of mind, so I stopped taking Paxil. Five weeks later, my memory came back, along with my worries. What remained was a firsthand experience of wearing rose-colored glasses, of seeing the world with new eyes.

Prozac Was the First SSRI

Prozac was the first member of a class of drugs known as selective serotonin reuptake inhibitors, or SSRIs. In what follows, I use Prozac to stand for the whole group, the psychological effects of which are nearly identical, and which includes Paxil, Zoloft, Celexa, Lexapro, and others. Many things are not known about Prozac and its cousins—above all, how they work. The name of the drug class tells part of the story: Prozac gets into the synapses (the gaps between neurons), but it is selective in affecting only synapses that use serotonin as their neurotransmitter. Once in the synapses, Prozac inhibits the reuptake process—the normal process in which a neuron that has just released serotonin into the synapse then sucks it back up into itself, to be released again at the next neural pulse. The net result is that a brain on Prozac has more serotonin in certain synapses, so those neurons fire more often.

So far Prozac sounds like cocaine, heroin, or any other drug that you might have learned is associated with a specific neurotransmitter. But the increase in serotonin happens within a day of taking Prozac, while the benefits don't appear for four to six weeks. Somehow, the neuron on the other side of the synapse is adapting to the new level of serotonin, and it is from that adaptation process that the benefits probably emerge. Or maybe neural adaptation has nothing to do with it. The other leading theory about Prozac is that it raises the level of a neural growth hormone in the hippocampus, a part of the brain crucial for learning and memory. People who have a negative affective style generally have higher levels of stress hormones in their blood; these hormones, in turn, tend to kill off or prune back some critical cells in the hippocampus, whose job, in part, is to shut off the very stress response that is killing them. So people who have a negative affective style may often suffer minor neural damage to the hippocampus, but this can be repaired in four or five weeks after Prozac triggers the release of the neural growth hormone. Although we don't know how Prozac works, we do know that it works: It produces benefits above placebo or no-treatment control groups on an astonishing variety of mental maladies, including depression, generalized anxiety disorder, panic attacks, social phobia, premenstrual dysphoric disorder, some eating disorders, and obsessive compulsive disorder.

Prozac Can Change Personalities with Ease

Prozac is controversial for at least two reasons. First, it is a shortcut. In most studies, Prozac turns out to be just about as effective as cognitive therapy—sometimes a little more, sometimes a little less—but it's so much easier than therapy. No daily homework or difficult new skills; no weekly therapy appointment. If you believe in the Protestant work ethic and the maxim "No pain, no gain," then you might be disturbed by Prozac. Second, Prozac does more than just relieve symptoms; it sometimes changes personality. In *Listening to Prozac*, Peter Kramer presents case studies of his patients whose long-standing depression or anxiety was cured by Prozac, and whose personalities then bloomed—greater self-confidence, greater resilience in the face of setbacks, and

Some case studies of patients with depression who were prescribed Prozac reveal that their personalities bloomed with greater self-confidence. (**Charlotte Wiig/Almay**)

more joy, all of which sometimes led to big changes in careers and relationships. These cases conform to an idealized medical narrative: person suffers from life-long disease; medical breakthrough cures disease; person released from shackles, celebrates new freedom; closing shot of person playing joyously with children; fade to black. But Kramer also tells fascinating stories about people who were not ill, who met no diagnostic category for a mental disorder, and who just had the sorts of neuroses and personality quirks that most people have to some degree—fear of criticism, inability to be happy when not in a relationship, tendency to be too critical and overcontrolling of spouse and children. Like all personality traits, these are hard to change, but they are what talk therapy is designed to address. Therapy can't usually change personality; but it can teach you ways of working around your problematic traits. Yet when Kramer prescribed Prozac, the offending traits went away. Lifelong habits, gone overnight (five weeks after starting Prozac), whereas years of psychotherapy often had done nothing. This is why Kramer coined the term "cosmetic psychopharmacology," for Prozac seemed to promise that psychiatrists could shape and perfect minds just as plastic surgeons shape and perfect bodies.

Why Not Change for the Better?

Does that sound like progress, or like Pandora's box? Before you answer that, answer this: Which of these two phrases rings truest to you: "Be all that you can be" or "This above all, to thine own self be true." Our culture endorses both—relentless self-improvement as well as authenticity—but we often escape the contradiction by framing self-improvement as authenticity. Just as gaining an education means struggling for twelve to twenty years to develop one's intellectual potential, character development ought to involve a lifelong struggle to develop one's moral potential. A nine-year-old child does

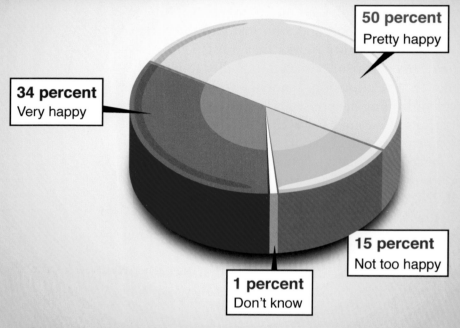

One-Third of Americans Are Very Happy

In a series of 3,014 telephone interviews conducted October 5– November 6, 2005, the Pew Research Center posed the following question: Generally, how would you say things are these days in your life? Would you say that you are very happy, pretty happy, or not too happy? The data gathered from the interview subjects, ages 18 years and older, appears below.

50 percent
Pretty happy

34 percent
Very happy

15 percent
Not too happy

1 percent
Don't know

Taken from: "Are We Happy Yet?" Pew Social Trends Reports, Pew Research Center, February 13, 2006.

not stay true to herself by keeping the mind and character of a nine-year-old; she works hard to reach her ideal self, pushed and chauffeured by her parents to endless after-school and weekend classes in piano, religion, art, and athletics. As long as change is gradual and a result of the child's hard work, the child is given the moral credit for the change, and that change is in the service of authenticity. But what if there were a pill that enhanced tennis skills? Or a minor surgical technique for implanting piano virtuosity directly and permanently into the brain?

Such a separation of self-improvement from authenticity would make many people recoil in horror.

Horror fascinates me, particularly when there is no victim. I study moral reactions to harmless taboo violations such as consensual incest and private flag desecration. These things just feel wrong to most people, even when they can't explain why. . . . My research indicates that a small set of innate moral intuitions guide and constrain the world's many moralities, and one of these intuitions is that the body is a temple housing a soul within. Even people who do not consciously believe in God or the soul are offended by or feel uncomfortable about someone who treats her body like a playground, its sole purpose to provide pleasure. A shy woman who gets a nose job, breast augmentation, twelve body piercings, and a prescription for elective Prozac would be as shocking to many people as a minister who remodels his church to look like an Ottoman harem.

The transformation of the church might hurt others by causing several parishioners to die from apoplexy [a stroke]. It is hard, however, to find harm in the self-transformer beyond some vague notion that she is "not being true to herself." But if this woman had previously been unhappy with her hypersensitive and overly inhibited personality, and if she had made little progress with psychotherapy, why exactly should she be true to a self she doesn't want? Why not change herself for the better? When I took Paxil, it changed my affective style for the better. It made me into something I was not, but had long wanted to be: a person who worries less, and who sees the world as being full of possibilities, not threats. Paxil improved the balance between my approach and withdrawal systems, and had there been no side effects, I would still be taking it today.

> **FAST FACT**
>
> In 2003 a World Values Survey of more then sixty-five countries ranked Nigeria number one in terms of happiness.

Prozac Can Help Restore Proper Function

I therefore question the widespread view that Prozac and other drugs in its class are overprescribed. It's easy for those who did well in the cortical lottery to preach about the importance of hard work and the unnaturalness of chemical shortcuts. But for those who, through no fault of their own, ended up on the negative half of the affective style spectrum, Prozac is a way to compensate for the unfairness of the cortical lottery. Furthermore, it's easy for those who believe that the body is a temple to say that cosmetic psychopharmacology is a kind of sacrilege. Something is indeed lost when psychiatrists no longer listen to their patients as people, but rather as a car mechanic would listen to an engine, looking only for clues about which knob to adjust next. But if the hippocampal theory of Prozac is correct, many people really do need a mechanical adjustment. It's as though they had been driving for years with the emergency brake halfway engaged, and it might be worth a five-week experiment to see what happens to their lives when the brake is released. Framed in this way, Prozac for the "worried well" is no longer just cosmetic. It is more like giving contact lenses to a person with poor but functional eyesight who has learned ways of coping with her limitations. Far from being a betrayal of that person's "true self," contact lenses can be a reasonable shortcut to proper functioning. . . .

Make It Available

Life is what we deem it, and our lives are the creations of our minds. But these claims are not helpful until augmented by a theory of the divided self . . . and an understanding of negativity bias and affective style. Once you know why change is so hard, you can drop the brute force method and take a more psychologically sophisticated approach to self-improvement. Buddha got it exactly right: You need a method for taming the elephant, for changing your mind gradually. Meditation, cognitive therapy, and Prozac are three effective means of doing so. Because each will be effective for some people and not for others, I believe that all three should be readily available and widely publicized. Life itself is but what you deem it, and you can—through meditation, cognitive therapy, and Prozac—redeem yourself.

Antidepressants Are Overprescribed

Deborah Kotz

In the following viewpoint Deborah Kotz contends that doctors may be prescribing too many antidepressants. Kotz talks with mental health professionals who believe that doctors are diagnosing depression and prescribing antidepressants to a significant number of people who are just experiencing normal sadness. Furthermore, Kotz says, when someone truly is afflicted with depression, doctors tend to use antidepressants as the "quick fix," even when psychotherapy or other treatments may be more appropriate. Kotz asserts that sadness is a normal emotional experience that should not be medicated away. Kotz is a widely published health journalist and coauthor of several health-related books.

D rugs may be an easy choice but not a good one. In the 19th-century novel *Hyperion*, Henry Wadsworth Longfellow admonished his hero, unlucky in love, to "take this sorrow to thy heart, and

SOURCE: Deborah Kotz, "The Right Rx for Sadness," *U.S. News & World Report*, vol. 143, July 29, 2007, pp. 58–61. Copyright © 2007 U.S. News and World Report, L.P. All rights reserved. Reprinted with permission.

make it a part of thee, and it shall nourish thee till thou art strong again." Had Paul Flemming been real and alive today, chances are he would have taken Prozac or Paxil instead. Last month [June 2007], the Centers for Disease Control and Prevention announced that antidepressants are the country's most commonly prescribed medication, accounting for 118 million prescriptions in 2005. A sign, some experts are wondering, that it's time to reassess?

Although many psychiatrists worry more about desperate souls not getting help, there's a growing concern that medicine often goes to people who shouldn't be taking

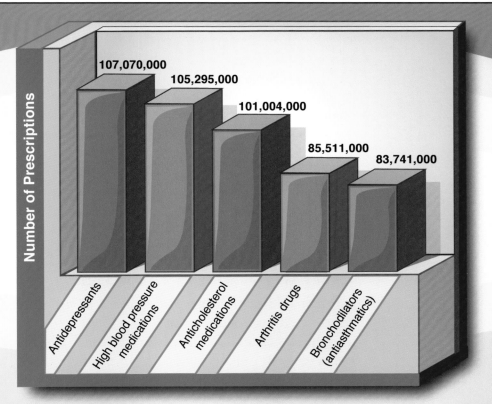

Five Most Frequently Prescribed Drugs at Doctor Office Visits in the United States, 2005

Number of Prescriptions

- Antidepressants: 107,070,000
- High blood pressure medications: 105,295,000
- Anticholesterol medications: 101,004,000
- Arthritis drugs: 85,511,000
- Bronchodilators (antiasthmatics): 83,741,000

Taken from: "National Ambulatory Medical Care Survey: 2005 Summary," U.S. Centers for Disease Control and Prevention, *Advance Data from Vital Health and Statistics*, no. 387, June 29, 2007. Table 25. www.cdc.gov/nchs/data/ad/ad387.pdf.

it. And a consensus has formed that the estimate of how many people will develop depression at some point—1 in 6—might be greatly inflated. "There's no question that the availability of these drugs has increased the diagnosis of depression," says Jerome Wakefield, a professor of social work at New York University. Wakefield is coauthor of the new book *The Loss of Sadness*, which argues that selective serotonin reuptake inhibitors [SSRIs]—Prozac, Paxil, Zoloft—are commonly overused to treat sadness, a normal and healthy response to divorce, sudden unemployment, the end of a friendship, a house foreclosure.

Flaws in Diagnostic Manual Lead to Overdiagnosis

The problem, experts say, may be flaws in the diagnostic manual mental-health professionals use to identify depression. "We need to figure out a way to come up with depression criteria that take into account the context in which symptoms develop," contends Robert Spitzer, professor of psychiatry at Columbia University, who helped produce various editions of the *Diagnostic and Statistical Manual of Mental Disorders* [*DSM*] and has concluded that it needs tweaking.

At the moment, only one such distinction is made. People grieving the death of a loved one, the manual allows, can temporarily exhibit all the signs of depression without having a mental illness. After two months, however, bereavement that lingers is classified as depression, even though mourning can go on much longer, says William Pollack, who teaches psychiatry at Harvard Medical School and is director of the Centers for Men at McLean Hospital. And severe sadness resulting from other traumas, doctors are left to conclude, must be clinical depression.

The loss factor. "We're starting to realize that it doesn't make sense to pull bereavement out of other losses," says Michael First, a research psychiatrist at the New York State

Psychiatric Institute and editor of the latest *DSM* manual, which defines depression as five or more of a constellation of nine symptoms—ranging from depressed mood and suicidal thoughts to fatigue, insomnia, and difficulty concentrating—that last for more than two weeks. The symptoms must be severe enough to interfere with the person's social life and normal activities and should not be caused by a condition like a low-functioning thyroid.

Now, a growing body of research suggests that change is in order. Wakefield and First published a study in April [2007] that found that prolonged depressive like symptoms are common in those experiencing broken hearts and other major life changes; after reviewing population surveys of 8,100 people, they discovered that nearly 25 percent of people who might fit the clinical definition of depression were actually showing normal signs of sadness. In 2001, about 10 percent of Manhattanites exhibited the symptoms of full-blown depression within the first two months after 9/11, [September 11, 2001, terrorist attacks] according to a survey conducted by New York Academy of Medicine researchers. That was nearly twice the rate expected in a normal population. And other researchers noted an 18 percent uptick in SSRI prescriptions among Medicaid patients living near the World Trade Center during those first few months. "These people were not medically disordered," argues Wakefield. "They probably needed support more than medication."

FAST FACT

In 1992–2002, 8 percent of U.S. adults reported taking an antidepressant within the last thirty days.

Antidepressants Are a Quick Fix

But primary-care physicians, who diagnose and treat the vast majority of depression cases, may be hard pressed to tease out the origin of symptoms during a quickie 10-minute physical. And without a blood test or brain scan for depression, doctors often rely on standard screening questionnaires to measure the symptoms themselves—which, like the *DSM* manual, don't consider the context in which they occur. The forms also don't take into account the impact that symptoms are having on a person's functioning, says Spitzer. That information would help indicate whether grief is progressing into a mental disorder.

Even when a life circumstance is found to be the culprit, doctors may be reluctant to refer patients to grief counselors or psychotherapists for emotional support. That's because managed care doesn't reimburse generously for therapy that entails more frequent and longer office visits, says Carolyn Robinowitz, president of the American Psychiatric Association. About 65 percent of employee health plans put a cap on the number of mental health visits, according to [health maintenance organization] Kaiser's 2006 survey of employer health benefits. And plenty of therapists don't accept insurance.

So what doctors often choose to do is write prescriptions. "It's the easy solution, especially when patients demand a quick fix," says Ellen McGrath, a psychologist in New York and author of *When Feeling Bad Is Good*. A 2005 study published in the *Journal of the American Medical Association* found that 55 percent of volunteers posing as patients with a few depression symptoms received a prescription for Paxil after saying they saw it advertised in a commercial; just 10 percent of those who did not ask for any antidepressants walked out with a prescription. Study leader Richard Kravitz, a professor of medicine at the University of California–Davis, says drug companies encourage this trend by bombarding consumers with ads that do not make enough of a distinction between sadness and depression.

Numbing Side Effects

But antidepressants are no panacea. While helping some sad folks numb the pain, they are known to tamp down joyous feelings, too. After being diagnosed with can-

cer several years ago, Barbara Kline of Corrales, N.M., sought antidepressants to help manage her fear of the disease and shock at having her professional life come to a grinding halt. But the 58-year-old public relations executive also found she wasn't able to feel any stirrings of pleasure—even from the masseuse who regularly came to her house. She decided to go off the meds after just four months. "I wanted to examine my feelings and then make something out of them," she says, which inspired her to start a cancer patient support group.

There are also side effects to consider. As many as 60 percent of SSRI users experience such sexual problems as decreased libido and erectile dysfunction, and about 25 percent have sleep difficulties, according to an April 2006 report published in the *Cleveland Clinic Journal of Medicine.* Young adults and teens face a slightly increased risk of suicidal thoughts during the first month of treatment, and new research suggests elderly users are at risk of accelerated bone loss.

Critics say that doctors are too willing to prescribe Prozac simply because their patients, influenced by advertising, are looking for a quick fix to their problems. **(Sally and Richard Greenhill/Alamy)**

Some experts also believe that medicating normal sadness could delay the healing process. "I'd always worn the busy mask, denying sadness, pretending I was happy," says Mark Linden O'Meara, who tried antidepressants without success to get over the deaths of his parents and severe financial troubles. "The drugs gave me headaches and made me feel so numb." The 49-year-old writer from Burnaby, British Columbia, says it took a long crying jag after a romantic breakup to help him finally start acknowledging the pain of his losses from years earlier. "As I released the emotion, I was eventually able to start laughing and enjoying life more."

Acknowledging Sadness

Designed to repair malfunctions of biochemical pathways in the brain, antidepressants aren't supposed to address the psychological source of sadness. "When antidepressants are given to those in mourning, their symptoms may go away, but they don't feel good," says Pollack. In some cases, though, medications can be vital: when grief intensifies to the point that someone, say, hallucinates or loses touch with reality. Or when a sad person gets stuck and moves into depression.

In most cases of sadness, feelings of anguish dissipate with enough time to process them. McGrath recommends a "feel, deal, heal" approach. She advises clients to acknowledge the depth of their despair and identify what triggered the feelings, then share the feelings with a close friend, family member, or therapist. As the sadness starts to lift, they integrate the episode into their life and appreciate how it has made them stronger. "So much of our society still feels [sadness] is a problem to be gotten rid of rather than understood and supported," Pollack says. Being open to the full complexity of human emotions, he adds, yields not just sadness but genuine happiness, too.

Electroconvulsive Therapy Can Help Those Who Are Depressed

Jane E. Brody

In the following viewpoint Jane E. Brody asserts that electroconvulsive therapy, or ECT, as physicians call it, can be an effective way to treat depression. Brody says that the ECT procedure has been improved since it was first used—frequently under inhumane and cruel conditions—in the 1930s. The improved procedure is gaining in popularity and can be an effective depression treatment for some people, she says. Brody is a *New York Times* health columnist, author, and speaker.

For an older woman I know who was suffering from "implacable depression" that refused to yield to any medications, electroconvulsive therapy—popularly called shock therapy—was a lifesaver. And Kitty Dukakis, wife of the former governor of Massachusetts and 1988 Democratic presidential nominee, says ECT, as doctors call it, gave her back her life, which had been rendered

SOURCE: Jane E. Brody, "Shock Therapy Loses Some of Its Shock Value," *New York Times*, September 19, 2006. Reprinted with permission.

nearly unlivable by unrelenting despair and the alcohol she used to assuage it. Neither woman has experienced the most common side effect of ECT: memory disruption, though Mrs. Dukakis recalls nothing of a five-day trip to Paris she took after her treatment.

The television host Dick Cavett, who also had the treatment, wrote in *People* magazine, "In my case, ECT was miraculous." Mr. Cavett added, "It was like a magic wand." But for a man I know who was suicidally depressed and given ECT as a last resort, it did nothing to relieve his depression but destroyed some of his long-term memory.

Such differences in effectiveness and side effects are not unusual in medicine and psychiatry, and they are not played down in a [2006] book called *Shock*, which Mrs. Dukakis wrote with Larry Tye, a former *Boston Globe* reporter. The book, in which Mrs. Dukakis details her experience with depression and ECT, explores the history, effectiveness and downsides of this nearly 70-year-old treatment, a remedy that has been repeatedly portrayed in film and literature as barbaric, inhuman, even torturous.

ECT's Comeback

Few people seem to know that ECT has undergone significant changes in recent decades, placing it more in line with widely accepted treatments like those used to restart a stopped heart or to correct an abnormal heart rhythm. After a rather precipitous decline in the 1960's when effective antidepressant drugs became available, ECT since the 1980's has experienced something of a comeback, and is used primarily in these circumstances:

- When rapid reversal of a severe or suicidal depression is needed.

- When depression is complicated by psychosis or catatonia.

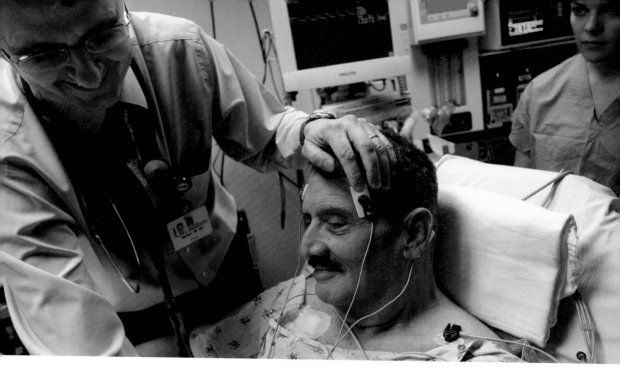

- When antidepressants and psychotherapy fail to alleviate a crippling depression.
- When antidepressants cannot safely be used, such as during pregnancy.
- When mania or bipolar disorder do not respond to drug therapy.

Though there is no official count, experts estimate that more than 100,000 patients undergo ECT each year in the United States.

ECT was developed in the 1930's by an Italian neurologist, Ugo Cerletti, who "tamed" difficult mental patients with electric shocks to the brain after noting that such shocks given to hogs before slaughter rendered them unconscious but did not kill them. In its first decades of use, ECT was administered to fully conscious patients, causing them to lose consciousness and experience violent seizures and uncontrolled muscle movements that sometimes broke bones. It was sometimes used in patients without their consent, or at least without informed consent.

And while evidence for its effectiveness did not extend much beyond depression, for a time ECT was applied to patients with all kinds of emotional disturbances, including schizophrenia. It was also widely used in mental hospitals to punish or sedate difficult patients, as was graphically depicted by Jack Nicholson in the movie *One Flew Over the Cuckoo's Nest*.

Some people may also recall that Ernest Hemingway, who suffered from life-long and often self-medicated depression, committed suicide in 1961 shortly after undergoing ECT. He had told his biographer: "Well, what is the sense of ruining my head and erasing my memory, which is my capital, and putting me out of business? It was a brilliant cure, but we lost the patient."

An Improved Procedure

Though the impression of ECT left in the public mind by such films and writings persists, ECT today is a far more refined and limited therapy. Most important, perhaps, is the use of anesthesia and muscle relaxants before administering the shock, which causes a 30-second convulsion in the brain without the accompanying movements. Thus, there is no physical damage. The pretreatment also leaves no memory of the therapy itself.

> **FAST FACT**
>
> It is estimated that between one hundred thousand and two hundred thousand patients undergo ECT in the United States every year.

The amount of current used today is lower and the pulse of electricity much shorter—about two seconds—reducing the risk of post-treatment confusion and memory disruption. While memory losses still occur in some patients, now the most serious risk associated with ECT is that of anesthesia.

Most patients require a series of six to eight treatments, delivered over several weeks. As my friend discovered, however, it is not universally effective. About three-fourths of patients are relieved of their debilitating symptoms at least temporarily. The remaining one-quarter are not helped, and some may be harmed.

Despite its long history, no one knows how ECT works to ease depression and mania. There is some evidence that it reorders the release of neurotransmitters, favoring an increase of substances like serotonin, which counters depression. Some experts view it as a pacemaker for the brain that disrupts negative circuitry.

The beauty of ECT is the speed with which it works. Antidepressants can take as long as six weeks to relieve serious depression. Mrs. Dukakis reported that she had begun to feel better after the first in an initial series of five outpatient ECT treatments given over a two-week period.

ECT Helps Wipe Away the Foreboding

But—and this is a big but—ECT is not a cure for depression. It is more like a stopgap measure that brings patients to a point where other approaches, including antidepressants and cognitive behavioral therapy, can work to stave off relapses. Although some ECT patients never relapse, most are like Mrs. Dukakis, who over the course of four years has come back for seven more rounds of ECT. She explained that while she used to deny the early signs of a recurring depression, she now calls her doctor "as soon as I spot the gathering clouds."

"ECT has wiped away that foreboding," she wrote, and "given me a sense of control, of hope." It has also helped her get off antidepressants, which had side effects like bowel, sexual and sleep disturbances and an inability to experience "the full range of my feelings."

ECT should not be administered without the patient's (or the patient's surrogate's) fully informed consent, which includes consideration of all possible side effects. The most common side effects are headache, muscle soreness and confusion shortly after the procedure, as well as short-term memory loss, which usually improves over a period of days to months.

Race and the Use of ECT

Percentage of Caucasian and African American patients with affective disorders admitted to the adult inpatient service of an academic medical center and treated using ECT, November 1993–March 2002:

Sex	Caucasian Patients (N=3,586)	African American Patients (N=1,657)
Male (N=2,027)	66.3%	33.7%
Female (N=3,216)	69.7%	30.3%

N = Number of patients

Taken from: William Breakey and Gary Dunn, "Racial Disparity in the Use of ECT for Affective Disorders," *American Journal of Psychiatry*, September 2004.

But according to the American Psychiatric Association, there is no evidence that ECT causes brain damage. Abuse of the procedure has declined strikingly. Today fewer than 2 percent of patients hospitalized in psychiatric facilities in New York State receive ECT. Properly used, it can be lifesaving.

Though there is not nearly the money to be made from ECT that there is in selling antidepressants, work on improvements continues. Modern ECT is sometimes delivered to only one side of the brain, reducing the chances of memory deficits.

Another new approach uses a magnetically induced current that can be aimed at specific regions of the brain, possibly altering them permanently. An advantage of this treatment, however, is that it does not require the use of anesthesia.

Electroconvulsive Therapy Is Harmful

Peter Breggin

In the following viewpoint Peter Breggin contends that electroconvulsive therapy (ECT) causes permanent brain damage and mental dysfunction. Breggin says a 2007 study led by an ECT proponent substantiates his argument. The study found adverse effects on the mental function of hundreds of patients six months after they had ECT treatments. According to Breggin, people who endure ECT treatments lose their sense of identity and mental life. Breggin, who has been fighting against ECT for several decades, says that shock treatments should be banned. Breggin is a psychiatrist, author, and founder of the International Center for the Study of Psychiatry and Psychology (ICSPP) and the journal Ethical Human Psychology and Psychiatry.

Something most remarkable and unexpected has occurred in the field of psychiatry. Led by a lifelong defender and promoter of shock treatment, Harold Sackeim, a team of investigators has recently [2007]

SOURCE: Peter Breggin, "Disturbing News for Patients and Shock Doctors Alike," *The Huffington Post*, April 1, 2007. Reproduced by permission.

published a follow up study of 347 patients given the currently available methods of electroshock, including the supposedly most benign forms—and confirmed that electroshock causes permanent brain damage and dysfunction.

Study Proves Damage

Based on numerous standardized psychological tests, six months after the last ECT [electroconvulsive therapy] every form of the treatment was found to cause lasting memory and mental dysfunction. In the summary words of the investigators, "Thus, adverse cognitive effects were detected six months following the acute treatment course." They concluded, "this study provides the first evidence in a large, prospective sample that adverse cognitive effects can persist for an extended period, and that they characterize routine treatment with ECT in community settings."

After traumatic brain damage has persisted for six months, it is likely to remain stable or even to grow worse. Therefore, the study confirms that routine clinical use of ECT causes permanent damage to the brain and its mental faculties.

The term cognitive dysfunction covers the entire range of mental faculties from memory to abstract thinking and judgment. The ECT-induced persistent brain dysfunction was global. In addition to the loss of autobiographical memories, the most marked cognitive injury occurred in "retention of newly learned information," "simple reaction time," and most tragically "global cognitive status" or overall mental function. In other words, the patients continued to have trouble learning and remembering new things, they were slower in their mental reaction times, and they were mentally impaired across a broad range of faculties.

Probably to disguise the wide swath of devastation, the Sackeim study did not provide the percentages of patients afflicted with persistent cognitive deficits; but all of the multiple tests were highly significant. . . . Also, the individual measures correlated with each other. This statistical data indicates that a large percentage of patients were significantly impaired.

Many patients also had persistent abnormalities on the EEGs (brain wave studies) six months after treatment, indicating even more gross underlying brain damage and dysfunction. The results confirm that the post-ECT patients, as I have described in numerous publications, were grossly brain-injured with a generalized loss of mental functions.

Some of the older forms of shock—*and still the most commonly used*—produced the most severe damage; but all of the treatment types caused persistent brain dysfunction. The greater the number of treatments given to patients, the greater was the loss of biographical memories. Elderly women are particularly likely to get shocked —probably because there is no one to defend them— and the study found that the elderly and females were the most susceptible to severe memory loss.

Destroying Lives

The study does not address the actual impact of these losses on the lives of individual patients. Like most such reports, it's all a matter of statistics. In human reality the loss of autobiographical memories indicates that patients could no longer recall important life experiences, such as their wedding, family celebrations, graduations, vacation trips, and births and deaths. In my experience, it also includes the wiping out of significant professional experiences. I have evaluated dozens of patients whose professional and family lives have been wrecked, including a nurse who lost her career but who recently [2005] won a malpractice suit against the doctor who referred her for shock. . . .

> **FAST FACT**
>
> From 2003 through 2007, people over age sixty-five have accounted for as much as 40 percent of ECT treatments conducted in Texas and California.

Complications from ECT in California, 1989–1994 (excluding 1993)

A total of 2,589 individuals, or 21 percent of all patients, suffered complications from electroconvulsive therapy.

Complication	Number of Patients	Percentage of All Patients
Cardiac arrest	6	0.04
Memory loss	2,424	19.7
Fractures	5	0.04
Apnea	154	1.25
Deaths	0	0.00

Taken from: California Department of Mental Health, figures as reported to the California State Legislature, 1989–1994 (1993 data not available). HealthyPlace.com.

Even when these injured people can continue to function on a superficial social basis, they nonetheless suffer devastation of their identities due to the obliteration of key aspects of their personal lives. The loss of the ability to retain and learn new material is not only humiliating and depressing but also disabling. The slowing of mental reaction time is frustrating and disabling. Even when relatively subtle, these disabilities can disrupt routine activities of living. Individuals can no longer safely drive a car for fear of losing their concentration or becoming hopelessly lost. Others can no longer find their way around their own kitchen or remember to turn off the burner on the stove. Still others cannot retain what they have just read in a newspaper or seen on television. They commonly meet old friends and new acquaintances without having any idea who they are. Ultimately, the experience of "global" cognitive dysfunction impairs the victim's identity and sense of self, as well as ruining the overall quality of life.

Although unmentioned in the Sackeim article, in addition to cognitive dysfunction, shock treatment causes severe affective or emotional disorders. Much like other victims of severe head injury, many post-shock patients become emotionally shallow and unable to relate on an intimate or spiritual level. They often become impulsive and irritable. Commonly they become chronically depressed. Having been injured by previously trusted doctors, they almost always become distrustful of all doctors and avoid even necessary medical care.

Decades of Opposition to Shock Treatment

This breaking scientific research has confirmed what I've been saying about shock treatment for thirty years. In 1979 I published *Electroshock: Its Brain-Disabling Effects*, the first medical book to evaluate the brain damaging and memory wrecking effects of this "treatment" for depression that requires inflicting a series of massive convulsions on the brain by means of passing a traumatic electric current through it. After many rejections, the courageous president of Springer Publishing Company, Ursula Springer, decided to publish this then controversial book. Dr. Springer told me about venomous attacks aimed at her at medical meetings as a result of her brave act in publishing my work. She never regretted it.

Over the years, I have continued to write, lecture, testify in court and speak to the media about brain damage and memory loss caused by electroshock. . . . At times my persistence has resulted in condemnation from shock advocates such as Harold Sackeim and Max Fink whom I have criticized for systematically covering up damage done to millions of patients throughout the world. It would require too much autobiographical detail to communicate the severity of the attacks on me surrounding my criticism of ECT. It was second only to the attack on me from the drug companies for claiming that antidepressants cause violence and suicide.

Given the vigor with which shock doctors have suppressed or denigrated my work, the study further surprised me by citing my 1986 scientific paper "Neuropathology and cognitive dysfunction from ECT" published in the *Psychopharmacology Bulletin*, noting that "critics contend that ECT invariably results in substantial and permanent memory loss." They contrast this critical view with "some authorities," specifically citing Max Fink and Robert Abrams, who have argued against the existence of any persistent shock effects on memory. The implication was clear that the critics were right and the so-called authorities were wrong. Sackeim was among those authorities.

Critics of electroconvulsive therapy say that the procedure often strips patients of important life experience memories. (Joe McNally/Getty Images)

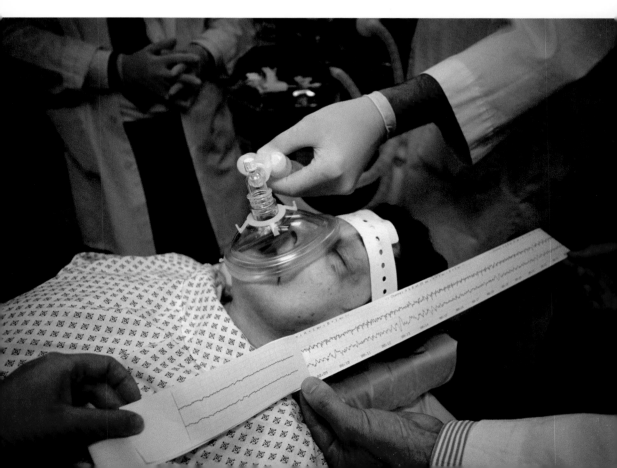

Fink's "authoritative" testimony at a number of malpractice trials has enabled shock doctors to get off Scott free after damaging the brains of their patients. Abrams used to testify successfully on behalf of shock doctors until I disclosed his ownership of a shock machine manufacturing company.

Unfortunately, the Sackeim group did not cite the work of neurologist John Friedberg who risked his career to criticize electroshock treatment. Nor did their article give credit to the published work of psychiatric survivor Leonard Frank or the anti-shock reform activities of the survivor movement led by David Oaks of MindFreedom. They also didn't cite Colin Ross's 2006 review and analysis showing that ECT is no more effective than sham ECT or simply sedating patients without shocking them.

Will the latest confirmation of ECT-induced brain damage cause shock doctors to cut back on their use of the treatment? Not likely. Psychiatrists and their affiliated neurosurgeons always knew that lobotomy was destroying the brains and mental life of their patients and that knowledge did not daunt them one bit. It required an organized international campaign to discredit, to slow down and to almost eliminate the surgical practice of psychiatric brain mutilation in the early 1970s. The ECT lobby is much larger and stronger than the lobotomy lobby, and much better organized, with its own journal and shock advocates positioned in high places in medicine and psychiatry. Stopping shock treatment will require public outrage, organized resistance from survivor groups and psychiatric reformers, lawsuits, and state legislation.

CHAPTER 3

Personal Stories

Depression:
My Hidden Disability

Adam Kahn

The following viewpoint is a transcript of a talk given by Stanford University student Adam Kahn to incoming freshmen in 2004. Kahn tells the students he may not look different on the outside, but inside he suffers from a hidden disability—bipolar disorder—which causes those afflicted to cycle between manic highs and depressive lows. Kahn describes how during his first few years at Stanford his illness got the better of him and forced him to withdraw from school. At home in New York his depression worsened until he finally took control of his disease and his life. He went back to Stanford and, with support and hard work, he achieved academic and personal success. Adam Kahn graduated from Stanford in 2006 with three degrees, a bachelor of arts, bachelor of science, and a master of arts.

L ook at me. I might not seem like your typical Faces of Community [Stanford program highlighting student diversity] speaker. I've sat in this audience twice—first as a freshman in Gavilan [dorm] and then as an OV [orientation volunteer]. People spoke on such

Photo on facing page. Many bipolar sufferers liken the effects of their disease to riding an emotional roller coaster with severe ups and downs. (Mikael Utterstrom/Alamy)

SOURCE: Adam Kahn, "Highs and Lows," from a speech delivered at Stanford University, September 23, 2004.

topics as being part of an ethnic minority, being gay, being physically disabled, etc. . . . and how these things have shaped their experiences in life and their time at Stanford.

So look at me. I'm white. I'm straight. I'm not in a wheelchair. At first you might think that the biggest minority category I fall into is that of a Yankee fan. I'm just your average New York Jew, so maybe I'm here to talk about that as a burden. It wouldn't be the first time a speaker at Faces of Community has talked about what it's like to be white, so maybe I'm here to offend you. But that's not the case. . . . I'm here to tell my story. What makes me different than most people on campus is what the staff at the Disability Resource Center [DRC] call a hidden disability.

I'm Bipolar

For the last five years I've been on a roller coaster ride of emotions with manic highs and depressive lows. I entered my senior year of high school at the top of my class. I ended it barely graduating. Depression made it impossible for me to complete my schoolwork on time, if at all. Though my senior year transcript looked a little bizarre, my college application still seemed to be strong enough for Stanford to take me. Had it not been such a miserable senior year for me, I might not have chosen Stanford. Upon visiting here after being accepted, I saw that this place was the embodiment of happiness, something I was lacking at the time.

When I came to Stanford, I thought my problems would all of a sudden disappear. Yes, being bipolar, I expected that psychologically things might not necessarily be a picnic, but I did expect them to remain just that—

psychological and in my head. Academically, I thought I'd be back to the person I was junior year of high school when nothing stood in my way of doing my schoolwork and doing it well. Unfortunately, I was wrong.

Difficult to Function

The fall of my freshman year was rough. I was overmedicated due to an incompetent psychiatrist back home and my new psychiatrist at Stanford Hospital was trying to rework my med load into something manageable. I was a zombie and could barely stay awake past 11 P.M. Meanwhile, I had a roommate who wanted to use our room as the preparty room every Friday and Saturday night. I was out of practice academically given my disastrous senior year of high school. I was still not turning my papers in on time. So I had to withdraw from an IntroSem [introductory seminar] and I failed IHUM [Introduction to Humanities] my first quarter here. Luckily, up until

Many students with bipolar disease find it difficult to concentrate on their studies. (Candice C. Cusic/MCT/Landov)

then, I never seemed to have problems with my techie stuff. For whatever reason, my mood didn't play a huge role in stopping me there. But lucky me had a Math 51H [an honors math class] final soon after I learned that I was going to fail IHUM, so I was so depressed that I ended up bombing a final in class that I had up until that point had an A in.

I thought the only help I needed was my psychiatrist at Stanford. The Disability Resource Center suggested I take a reduced course load, an option that is open to students with all types of disabilities. My parents wanted me in psychotherapy since my psychiatrist only did med management. But no—I thought I was still the same Adam from a few years before who could do anything academically he wanted.

I remained in an academic holding pattern for the next two years. Every quarter I would get at least one incomplete. I usually finished them, but I did not have a single vacation from school where I did not have some work to make up. I had to withdraw from my PWR [program in writing and rhetoric] so I had to take a writing course at a state school back home over the summer. Even there, I had a lot of trouble finishing my work on time. But I thought my mood was getting better and that my medications were controlling things better. I briefly tried some psychotherapy but felt that it wasn't that helpful. As long as I was getting my work done and completed my incompletes, I thought I'd be fine eventually. In my mind each quarter I thought "Next quarter things will be back to normal." And with every quarter came incompletes.

And then came the spring of my sophomore year. I took one too many incompletes. I was taking 17 units, but only completed 8 by the end of the quarter. So I got a letter in the mail saying I was on Academic Probation. I didn't worry much. I thought I'd get the incompletes done and it would take me off probation. I also thought I wouldn't have any academic problems in the future and that I would catch up on everything over the summer and be back in the fall like nothing ever happened.

I still entered the fall of my junior year having 4 incompletes, one which would turn into a failing grade if I didn't finish it by the end of the quarter. I finally took the advice of the Disability Resource Center and took a reduced courseload. I started working with a writing tutor provided by the DRC. I started psychotherapy again. And I thought I'd be fine because I was finally on a perfect med regiment that made me the happiest I was in a long time. My mood would be fine so why not my academics?

Forced to Withdraw, My Depression Worsens

But it was too late at that point. The anxiety of all the remaining incompletes piled up and despite the fact that I wasn't depressed, I was too anxious to finish the quarter. Therefore I had to withdraw from both my classes. Therefore I completed 0 units. Therefore Academic Standing decided to skip over the second warning that most people get, and instead placed me on a one year academic suspension.

Let's pause for a second and ask a question. Am I supposed to be a role model for you all? Why would the school want somebody who bombed academically, failed IHUM, and ended up suspended speak to the entire freshman class on this stage? My guess is because I am here to stand on this stage. During my suspension, at first my depression spiraled downhill. I was stuck at home during one of the coldest winters in New York history, my depression getting worse and worse.

After being home for four months, things were so bad that my parents made me enter a continuing day treatment program where I would spend my mornings in intensive group therapy at a local psychiatric hospital.

There I encountered people with problems even greater than mine. Many people in the program suffered from borderline personality disorder. Many heard voices in their head or at times had hallucinations. I've never used drugs or alcohol, whereas most patients had a history of substance abuse. I realized that despite my problems, I was one of the lucky ones. The treatment program focused on thinking about the "here and now." And for most of these people, their "here and now" was much worse than mine. And in terms of the future, they didn't have a Stanford to look forward to returning to.

I Learned to Take Control of My Life

At times it felt like I would never make it back to the Farm [nickname for Stanford]. At times it felt like I was too far gone. Slowly, but surely, with the skills I was being taught in treatment, I learned to take control of my life. I was able to complete some of the incompletes from home. I was able to prove to the school that I was well enough to return a quarter early from my suspension. More importantly, I was able to prove to myself that I was well enough to return a quarter early from my suspension. The school made an exception and let me do just that.

So I came back to campus last fall with the burden of knowing that if I were to screw up again, I'd be placed on a three year academic suspension. I was nervous. But I was ready to face the challenge. But this time around I took a reduced course load and entered psychotherapy immediately. I pulled off a mighty fine fall quarter turning all my work in on time for the first time in over four years. Winter quarter, I took a risk. I took a full course load. I pulled that off pretty nicely as well.

Because of all my success, I was no longer afraid to take risks and put myself out there. I wasn't afraid of taking classes outside my comfort zone. Socially, I took risks as well. Unlike most guys at Stanford, I wasn't afraid to ask girls out on dates. I might not have had the best luck with this, but I took these risks nonetheless, something all of you, both male and female, should do. Take it from me; there are a lot of scarier things in life to fear than rejection. I can take risks and do things I never would have done before because I have finally taken control over my life and realize what a wonderful life it is. Taking a risk entails sacrificing who you are for what you might become, and I am so excited to see what I might become.

I'd be lying if I said life is easy for me. My bipolar disorder does a lot to make me who I am. On the other hand, it is not who I am. It does not define me like it once did. When I joked with a friend about how I was speaking today about being crazy, she said Adam, "I know you're crazy, but there are many more things than just one that make you who are, and they all count." You know what? I couldn't agree with her more. Yes, at the end of the day, I'm still bipolar, but with the support I've received along the way, I've changed so much and I'm in a position where I can stand on this stage and tell you my story knowing how great the present is and how great the future can be.

No Shame in Having a Mental Illness

I chose Stanford because I thought it embodied happiness. It does. But at the same time, it has what many people here refer to as the duck metaphor. Everybody seems wonderful above the surface, but underneath, we're all just paddling to stay afloat. Some people paddle more than others. I once paddled more than most of you will ever or should ever have to paddle. You might be sitting next to somebody who is bipolar or suffers from depression. Your roommate might be a cutter or suffer from an eating disorder. Don't be afraid to make sure that they are okay and if they need help. And if you are paddling as much as I was, don't be afraid to ask for help. There are many places for support. There's Vaden [Health Center] and CAPS [Counseling and Psychological Services], there's the Disability Resource Center, there's The Bridge [a peer counseling center], there's your residence staff, there's your friends. Utilize them. Don't wait until you're suspended like I was to ask for help. For those of you who have hidden disabilities like me, do all you can so one day you can stand on this stage, tell your story, and tell everybody about the risks you've taken along the way.

You may disagree with me when I say there's no shame in being a Yankee fan, but I can tell you with all my heart, there is no shame in suffering from mental illness. Thank you. Welcome to Stanford, Class of '08.

Postpartum Depression Is a Cruel Condition

Alex Winter

The following viewpoint is written by Alex Winter, a mother who suffered through postpartum depression (PPD). Winter discusses the first few days after bringing her son home from the hospital. This is supposed to be a time of great joy in a new mother's life, but Winter felt anything but joyful. She did not want anything to do with her new son. Eventually she was diagnosed with PPD. After treatment with the antidepressant Prozac, her condition improved. Two years after the birth of her son, she is telling her story to help others understand PPD. Winter is a psychiatric nurse and writer.

Postpartum depression (PPD) is a cruel condition that affects new mothers shortly after childbirth. It is not the "baby blues." It is pervasive, it is overwhelming, and it is debilitating. PPD strips women of the joys normally associated with a new baby, leaving them with feelings of frustration and guilt.

SOURCE: Alex Winter, "Testimonies, Postpartum Depression from an Individual Perspective," Helium.com, 2007. Reproduced by permission.

"I Didn't Want to Be a Mother"

As a psychiatric nurse, I had much experience helping clients suffering from PPD. However, I did not fully appreciate its horrific symptoms and effects on one's psyche until I fell victim after the birth of my son. I remember coming home from the hospital on a beautiful spring day and all I felt as I gazed at the flowers in bloom was a bone-deep sadness. I didn't want to go inside to my baby. I wanted to take it all back. I didn't want to be a mother . . . I didn't want my son.

The first night at home was horrible. The baby didn't sleep well, as was to be expected. Adding the lack of sleep

Postpartum depression symptoms can cause a woman to reject her baby.
(Jennifer Brown/Alamy)

to my frayed state of continuous panic was devastating. I began having disturbing physical symptoms such as nausea and vomiting, diarrhea, and abdominal pains. I went to the emergency room, where my wonderful obstetrician, who'd been in practice over 30 years, came to see me. He was very concerned about my symptoms, which I didn't understand. After all, wasn't this just, perhaps, a bowel obstruction caused by my C-section? A simple fix . . . I would be hospitalized for weeks and my husband's family would take care of the baby. I am appalled as I write my story that a life-threatening intestinal condition was actually the superior alternative to caring for my own child.

> **FAST FACT**
>
> According to the American College of Obstetricians and Gynecologists, about 10 percent of new mothers suffer from postpartum depression, while 70 percent experience the "baby blues."

Diagnosis: Postpartum Depression

When I read my ER discharge papers I was shocked to discover I had been diagnosed with anxiety, fatigue, and PPD. What? Where was the bowel obstruction? The abdominal adhesions? That I, as a mental health professional, tried in vain to lend physical credence to my psychological symptoms is, in and of itself, a testament to the stigma that remains in our society about mental illness.

After a few days of worsening physical and emotional symptoms, which included suicidal ideation and a true desire to give my child up for adoption, I was placed on Prozac. The PPD gradually improved, but I remained on the medication for over 6 months. My doctor told me mine was the worst case of PPD he'd seen in his many years of practice. I've seen much worse in all my years of practice. My belief is many women are ashamed of the feelings and inadequacies associated with PPD, and therefore don't discuss their symptoms with their providers, or even their family members. I propose that this condition, brought on by deviated levels of hormones already out-of-balance due to the tolls of pregnancy, is much more common than what is demonstrated by the statistics. In addition, I believe the effects of PPD on the lives of new mothers, their infants, and their loved ones is much more extensive.

Telling My Story

My son is now over 2 years old. He is beautiful, he is funny, and he is full of life and mischief and love. I feel incredibly blessed. But I would be remiss if I didn't admit to feelings of shame, and of anger. How could I have had those horrible thoughts about motherhood and my own precious child? Why couldn't I have been allowed the ability to enjoy those precious first months of my son's life? Those moments will forever be a haze for me, cast in shadow and cloaked in sorrow.

No matter how I wish to change the past, I can't. Even if I traveled back in time, I couldn't have done anything differently. What I have come to accept is that PPD is an illness. I didn't ask for it. I couldn't prevent it. But I can tell my story in an attempt to help others understand the emotional, physical, and spiritual crisis that is postpartum depression.

Turning Tragedy into Greater Awareness for Depression

Al Kluesner

In the following viewpoint Al Kluesner writes about the suicide deaths of two of his children. The circumstances surrounding Amy and Michael Kluesner's suicides were different. Amy suicided, as Kluesner says, a few months before she would have graduated from college. She died without anyone really knowing she suffered and without ever having a chance for treatment. If Amy would have received treatment and had the support of those around her, Kluesner believes she would have been able to fight her depression. Michael took his life at the age of thirty-eight, despite having been treated for over ten years. Still, Kluesner wonders if Michael could have been saved if he had tried lithium or electroconvulsive therapy. Kluesner hopes that by educating others about depression and the many treatments available, he may be able to prevent suicide and spare other families the pain of losing a loved one. Al Kluesner and his wife, Mary, along with other parents who have lost children to suicide, started the organization Suicide Awareness Voices of Education (SAVE) to educate the public about suicide prevention.

SOURCE: Al Kluesner, "Two Suicides: The Difference It Makes," Suicide Awareness Voices of Education, 2003–2007. Reproduced by permission.

My son Michael suicided on March 22, 1997 at age 38 just eight days and twelve years after my daughter Amy's suicide on March 30, 1985. One wonders how a person can handle such tragedies. What else can one do but just cope, and play out the hand dealt to them. The difference between Amy's suicide and Michael's was we were totally blindsided by Amy whereas Michael had been treated for depression for over ten years and was later diagnosed with manic depression. Michael was living at our home, a nurturing and close environment, when he suicided; Amy died alone. What difference does it make—dead is dead!

We Never Knew Amy Was Sick

The difference is that Michael had many people who loved and worked with him to try to stop this terrible brain disease that was spiraling his life downward to the deepest of black holes. Amy was also trying to stop the same deadly spiral but had few if any people helping her. What difference does it make? For some reason I believe that Amy may have been able to control her brain disease if she and the people around her only knew what was happening. After spending a semester at Providence College, she transferred to Iowa State University to study Entomology. She was one of only nineteen other undergraduate students in the department. Amy had a 3.9 GPA in college and was ready to graduate in June of 1985. In high school, Amy played soccer and was a cheerleader. One of her favorite past times was playing the flute; she always played first or second chair. The last time I heard Amy play was at her brother Kevin's wedding. Her other brothers Michael and Philip were ushers at the wedding.

The family was doing just great—in fact fabulous. Kevin, a graduate of the University of St. Johns, recently

> **FAST FACT**
>
> According to the World Health Organization, fewer than 25 percent of those affected with depression worldwide have access to effective treatments.

returned from South Africa where he worked after a short stint in New York City. Philip, a graduate of Saint Mary's University just received the highest all around award as "Redman of the Year" from Saint Mary's and was off to teach and coach at a high school in New Hampshire. Michael recently transferred from Stetson College in Florida to the University of Wisconsin in Madison where upon graduation he was offered a position as a teacher's assistant in the communications and German departments. He refused and decided to come home to Minneapolis.

This is the way life should have remained; we learned to ski, canoe and play tennis together, we vacationed together from Nantucket Island to Vermont, from Florida to Colorado and we went to church together. But things

Many suicides could be prevented if family members were aware that a loved one is suffering from depression and could encourage that person to seek therapy. (**Photofusion Picture Library/Alamy**)

were to change suddenly and drastically. On March 28, 1985 my wife Mary and I received a letter from Amy. It was a buoyant upbeat letter with a handwriting style full of flourish. This handwriting style was quite different for Amy but at that moment I felt very happy—things seemed to be going well for her. We gave the university a high school girl and our daughter was returning as a confident young woman. I was excited to catch the plane and meet up with Mary in Florida. We also had tickets to a horse jumping show in Tampa. Two days later when we returned from the horse show, we had a phone call from our son Kevin—Amy suicided. She was in the back seat of the family car with her Raggedy Ann doll and her favorite blanket. I couldn't accept it, it was too cold in the house; she slept in the car to get warm. At that point, our lives changed and would change again.

He Had the Best Team of Doctors— and Still We Lost Him

In January 1997 Mary knew that Michael's depression was deepening despite the treatment. She knew that we were losing Michael. Five weeks before his death she said to me that she didn't think Michael would make it. I didn't agree because he had the best team of doctors, psychiatrists, psychologists and mental health counselors in Minneapolis. He was hospitalized four weeks earlier—and still we lost him. Mary was with Michael at the last session with his doctors. He cried openly at that time pointing out that "the pain is too great." When asked why he didn't suicide, he said "I can't do it because of my family." He had struggled with alcohol and drugs since high school. Michael's depression was "early onset" but he was not medically treated until he was 30 years old. Depression robbed Michael of personal relationships, good jobs, good humor, grace and social ease. When his depression eased up he was charming, caring, social and lovable. This was Michael's letter to us written one day before he suicided.

To my family: I don't understand how a loving God would allow my head to be filled with such terrible thoughts all the time. Ever since coming out of the hospital the world has seemed like cardboard, as if all the faces and everything I see aren't "right," that death is around me much of the time. What is God trying to prove? It's horrible and I didn't want to fully admit how bad it is. I didn't want to end up in the hospital as a psychotic. I've had a couple of good days here and there. The medication seemed to help for a little while, but nothing is taking away this feeling that the world is a freaky place where I don't belong. The job interviews and phone calls and everyday conversations I have feel forced, unnatural, creepy. I'm not blaming the medical community. They did the best they could, but the doctors really don't understand what it's like to live this way 24 hours a day. This brain disease is hideous for those of us seriously affected. The genetic factor is huge. We understand so little about it. Please forgive me. I can't go on like this. It's too horrible. I'm sorry I plan to use alcohol at the very end. I don't want to go to the hospital again. I'm sure I would feel the same if I had a great job and a great marriage. This is a chemical disorder that has been worsening over the years. I believe God has a reason for this, mysterious as it is, and that He has a place for me that is peaceful. I love you all very much.

4:15 P.M. 3/21/97
Love, Michael

Mike bought a used rifle, twelve bullets, and then drove his van to a beautiful park by a lake and shot himself at approximately 3:00 P.M. on March 22, 1997.

Lithium and Electro Convulsive Therapy were treatments not used for Michael who was suffering from manic depression which was diagnosed late in his illness. Perhaps these treatments would have helped. In Amy's case her school had some indication that she was having trouble but we were never told. She never had a chance for treatment that might have made a difference.

Helping Others Eases Our Grief

In response to our grief Mary and I, along with five other couples, started the organization Suicide Awareness Voices of Education (SAVE) two years after Amy's death to publicly speak out for suicide survivors and to educate the public about suicide prevention. SAVE is dedicated to public awareness programs that encourage the identification and treatment of depression and the elimination of the stigma often associated with the illness and with suicide. The organization is based in Minneapolis and has developed a billboard and poster awareness campaign for the local community. Recently, SAVE started a pilot program in Cleveland with AFSP-NE Ohio [American Foundation for Suicide Prevention of Northeast Ohio] and has been developing sponsorship to expand its message across the U.S. Ad slicks on suicide prevention are provided to over 1500 college newspapers today. To date these ads have appeared in many newspapers including, Columbia, Harvard, Stanford, and Purdue.

Recently, I had an experience that I feel illustrates SAVE's mission. I had mentioned to my local barber that I was on my way to New York to attend AFSP's Lifesavers Dinner. In our conversation she revealed to me that her father had suffered for fourteen years from the complications of a severe depression that had had a devastating impact on their family. No one in the family realized that their father was suffering from a treatable illness. He is now receiving treatment and his life and their lives have changed dramatically for the better. It is our hope that by educating the public about depression we can eliminate needless suffering and in some cases prevent suicide. That educational message does not eliminate the big hole—the cavity that will always remain with me and the rest of our family—but it does help.

VIEWPOINT 4

Antidepressants Saved My Life

Chris Rose

In the following viewpoint Chris Rose describes his descent into depression and the medication that finally pulled him out of it. As a journalist writing for the *Times-Picayune*, a New Orleans newspaper, Rose was compelled to tell the story of post-Katrina New Orleans. Unfortunately, the despair and heartache he wrote about seemed to engulf him, and he spiraled into depression. After prodding from family and friends, Rose finally sought help and was prescribed an antidepressant. After a few days he rediscovered his life again. Rose is a columnist for the *Times-Picayune*.

I pulled into the Shell station on Magazine Street, my car running on fumes. I turned off the motor. And then I just sat there.

There were other people pumping gas at the island I had pulled into and I didn't want them to see me, didn't want to see them, didn't want to nod hello, didn't want to interact in any fashion.

SOURCE: Chris Rose, "Hell and Back," *New Orleans Times-Picayune*, October 22, 2006. Copyright © 2008 The Times-Picayune Publishing Co. All rights reserved. Used with permission of The Times-Picayune.

PERSPECTIVES ON DISEASES AND DISORDERS   131

Outside the window, they looked like characters in a movie. But not my movie.

I tried to wait them out, but others would follow, get out of their cars and pump and pay and drive off, always followed by more cars, more people. How can they do this, like everything is normal, I wondered. Where do they go? What do they do?

It was early August and two minutes in my car with the windows up and the air conditioner off was insufferable. I was trapped, in my car and in my head.

So I drove off with an empty tank rather than face strangers at a gas station.

· · · · · · · ·

Before I continue this story, I should make a confession. For all of my adult life, when I gave it thought —which wasn't very often—I regarded the concepts of depression and anxiety as pretty much a load of hooey.

I never accorded any credibility to the idea that such conditions were medical in nature. Nothing scientific about it. You get sick, get fired, fall in love, get laid, buy a new pair of shoes, join a gym, get religion, seasons change—whatever; you go with the flow, dust yourself off, get back in the game. I thought anti-depressants were for desperate housewives and fragile poets.

I no longer feel that way. Not since I fell down the rabbit hole myself and enough hands reached down to pull me out.

One of those hands belonged to a psychiatrist holding a prescription for anti-depressants. I took it. And it changed my life.

Maybe saved my life.

This is the story of one journey—my journey—to the edge of the post-Katrina abyss, and back again. It is a story with a happy ending—at least so far.

· · · · · · · ·

I had already stopped going to the grocery store weeks before the Shell station meltdown. I had made every excuse possible to avoid going to my office because I didn't want to see anyone, didn't want to engage in small talk, hey, how's the family?

My hands shook. I had to look down when I walked down the steps, holding the banister to keep steady. I was at risk every time I got behind the wheel of a car; I couldn't pay attention.

I lost 15 pounds and it's safe to say I didn't have a lot to give. I stopped talking to Kelly, my wife. She loathed me, my silences, my distance, my inertia.

I stopped walking my dog, so she hated me, too. The grass and weeds in my yard just grew and grew.

I stopped talking to my family and my friends. I stopped answering phone calls and e-mails. I maintained limited communication with my editors to keep my job but I started missing deadlines anyway.

My editors, they were kind. They cut me slack. There's a lot of slack being cut in this town now. A lot of legroom, empathy and forgiveness.

I tried to keep an open line of communication with my kids to keep my sanity, but it was still slipping away. My two oldest, 7 and 5, began asking: "What are you looking at, Daddy?"

The thousand-yard stare. I couldn't shake it. Boring holes into the house behind my back yard. Daddy is a zombie. That was my movie: Night of the Living Dead. Followed by Morning of the Living Dead, followed by Afternoon. . . .

· · · · · · · ·

My own darkness first became visible last fall [2007]. As the days of covering the Aftermath [of Hurricane

Katrina] turned into weeks which turned into months, I began taking long walks, miles and miles, late at night, one arm pinned to my side, the other waving in stride. I became one of those guys you see coming down the street and you cross over to get out of the way.

I had crying jags and fetal positionings and other "episodes." One day last fall, while the city was still mostly abandoned, I passed out on the job, fell face first into a tree, snapped my glasses in half, gouged a hole in my forehead and lay unconscious on the side of the road for an entire afternoon.

You might think that would have been a wake-up call, but it wasn't. Instead, like everything else happening to me, I wrote a column about it, trying to make it all sound so funny.

It probably didn't help that my wife and kids spent the last four months of 2005 at my parents' home in Maryland. Until Christmas I worked, and lived, completely alone.

Even when my family finally returned, I spent the next several months driving endlessly through bombed-out neighborhoods. I met legions of people who appeared to be dying from sadness, and I wrote about them.

I was receiving thousands of e-mails in reaction to my stories in the paper, and most of them were more accounts of death, destruction and despondency by people from around south Louisiana. I am pretty sure I possess the largest archive of personal Katrina stories, little histories that would break your heart.

I guess they broke mine.

I am an audience for other people's pain. But I never considered seeking treatment. I was afraid that medication would alter my emotions to a point of insensitivity, lower my antenna to where I would no longer feel the acute grip that Katrina and the flood have on the city's psyche.

I thought, I must bleed into the pages for my art. Talk about "embedded" journalism, this was the real deal.

Worse than chronicling a region's lamentation, I thought, would be walking around like an ambassador from Happy Town telling everybody that everything is just fine, carry on, chin up, let a smile be your umbrella.

As time wore on, the toll at home worsened. I declined all dinner invitations that my wife wanted desperately to accept, something to get me out of the house, get my feet moving. I let the lawn and weeds overgrow and didn't pick up my dog's waste. I rarely shaved or even bathed. I stayed in bed as long as I could, as often as I could. What a charmer I had become.

I don't drink anymore, so the nightly self-narcolepsy that so many in this community employ was not an option. And I don't watch TV. So I developed an infinite capacity to just sit and stare. I'd noodle around on the piano, read weightless fiction and reach for my kids, always, trying to hold them, touch them, kiss them.

Tell them I was still here.

But I was disappearing fast, slogging through winter and spring and grinding to a halt by summer. I was a dead man walking.

I had never been so scared in my life.

. . . .

Early this summer [2006] with the darkness clinging to me like my own personal humidity, my stories in the newspaper moved from gray to brown to black. Readers wanted stories of hope, inspiration and triumph, something to cling to; I gave them anger and sadness and gloom. They started e-mailing me, telling me I was bringing them down when they were already down enough.

This one, Aug. 21, from a reader named Molly: "I recently became worried about you. I read your column and you seemed so sad. And not in a fakey-columnist kind of way."

This one, Aug. 19, from Debbie Koppman: "I'm a big fan. But I gotta tell ya—I can't read your columns anymore. They are depressing. I wish you'd write about something positive."

There were scores of e-mails like this, maybe hundreds. I lost count. Most were kind—solicitous, even; strangers invited me over for a warm meal.

But, this one, on Aug. 14 from a reader named Johnny Culpepper, stuck out: "Your stories are played out Rose. Why don't you just leave the city, you're not happy, you bitch and moan all the time. Just leave or pull the trigger and get it over with."

I'm sure he didn't mean it literally—or maybe he did, I don't know—but truthfully, I thought it was funny. I showed it around to my wife and editors.

Three friends of mine have, in fact, killed themselves in the past year and I have wondered what that was like. I rejected it. But, for the first time, I understood why they did it.

Hopeless, helpless and unable to function. A mind shutting down and taking the body with it. A pain not physical but not of my comprehension and always there, a buzzing fluorescent light that you can't turn off.

No way out, I thought. Except there was.

· · · · · · · ·

I don't need to replay the early days of trauma for you here. You know what I'm talking about.

Whether you were in south Louisiana or somewhere far away, in a shelter or at your sister's house, whether you lost everything or nothing, you know what I mean.

Then again, my case is less extreme than the first responders, the doctors and nurses and EMTs, and certainly anyone who got trapped in the Dome or the Convention Center or worse—in the water, in their attics and on their rooftops. In some cases, stuck in trees.

I've got nothing on them. How the hell do they sleep at night?

So none of this made sense. My personality has always been marked by insouciance and laughter, the seeking of adventure and new experiences. I am the class clown, the life of the party, the bon vivant.

I have always felt like I was more alert and alive than anyone in the room.

In the measure of how one made out in the storm, my life was cake. My house, my job and my family were all fine. My career was gangbusters; all manner of prestigious awards and attention. A book with great reviews and stunning sales, full auditoriums everywhere I was invited to speak, appearances on TV and radio, and the overwhelming support of readers who left gifts, flowers and cards on my doorstep, thanking me for my stories.

I had become a star of a bizarre constellation. No doubt about it, disasters are great career moves for a man in my line of work. So why the hell was I so miserable? This is the time of my life, I told myself. I am a success. I have done good things.

To no avail.

I changed the message on my phone to say: "This is Chris Rose. I am emotionally unavailable at the moment. Please leave a message."

I thought this was hilarious. Most of my friends picked it up as a classic cry for help.

My editor, my wife, my dad, my friends and just strangers on the street who recognized me from my picture in the paper had been telling me for a long time: You need to get help.

I didn't want help. I didn't want medicine. And I sure as hell didn't want to sit on a couch and tell some guy with glasses, a beard and a psych degree from Dartmouth all about my troubles.

Everybody's got troubles. I needed to stay the course, keep on writing, keep on telling the story of this city. I needed to do what I had to do, the consequences be damned, and what I had to do was dig further and further into what has happened around here—to the people, my friends, my city, the region.

Lord, what an insufferable mess it all is.

I'm not going to get better, I thought. I'm in too deep.

. . . .

In his book *Darkness Visible: A Memoir of Madness* —the best literary guide to the disease that I have found— the writer William Styron recounted his own descent into and recovery from depression, and one of the biggest obstacles, he said, was the term itself, what he calls "a true wimp of a word."

He traces the medical use of the word "depression" to a Swiss psychiatrist named Adolf Meyer, who, Styron said, "had a tin ear for the finer rhythms of English and therefore was unaware of the damage he had inflicted by offering 'depression' as a descriptive noun for such a dreadful and raging disease.

"Nonetheless, for over 75 years the word has slithered innocuously through the language like a slug, leaving little trace of its intrinsic malevolence and preventing, by its very insipidity, a general awareness of the horrible intensity of the disease when out of control."

He continued: "As one who has suffered from the malady in extremis yet returned to tell the tale, I would lobby for a truly arresting designation. 'Brainstorm,' for instance, has unfortunately been preempted to describe, somewhat jocularly, intellectual inspiration. But something along these lines is needed.

"Told that someone's mood disorder has evolved into a storm—a veritable howling tempest in the brain, which is indeed what a clinical depression resembles like nothing else—even the uninformed layman might display sympathy rather than the standard reaction that 'depression' evokes, something akin to 'So what?' or 'You'll pull out of it' or 'We all have bad days.'"

Styron is a helluva writer. His words were my life. I was having one serious brainstorm. Hell, it was a brain hurricane, Category 5. But what happens when your own personal despair starts bleeding over into the lives of those around you?

What happens when you can't get out of your car at the gas station even when you're out of gas? Man, talk about the perfect metaphor.

Then this summer, a colleague of mine at the newspaper took a bad mix of medications and went on a violent driving spree Uptown, an episode that ended with his pleading with the cops who surrounded him with guns drawn to shoot him.

He had gone over the cliff. And I thought to myself: If I don't do something, I'm next.

. . . .

My psychiatrist asked me not to identify him in this story and I am abiding by that request.

I was referred to him by my family doctor. My first visit was Aug. 15 [2006]. I told him I had doubts about his ability to make me feel better. I pled guilty to skepticism about the confessional applications of his profession and its dependency medications.

I'm no Tom Cruise; psychiatry is fine, I thought. For other people.

My very first exchange with my doctor had a morbidly comic element to it; at least, I thought so, but my sense of humor was in delicate balance to be sure.

While approaching his office, I had noticed a dead cat in his yard. Freshly dead, with flies just beginning to gather around the eyes. My initial worry was that some kid who loves this cat might see it, so I said to him: "Before we start, do you know about the cat?"

Yes, he told me. It was being taken care of. Then he paused and said: "Well, you're still noticing the environment around you. That's a good sign."

The analyst in him had already kicked in. But the patient in me was still resisting. In my lifelong habit of dampening down any serious discussion with sarcasm, I said to him: "Yeah, but what if the dead cat was the only thing I saw? What if I didn't see or hear the traffic or the trees or the birds or anything else?"

I crack myself up. I see dead things. Get it?

Yeah, neither did he.

We talked for an hour that first appointment. He told me he wanted to talk to me three or four times before he made a diagnosis and prescribed an antidote. When I came home from that first visit without a prescription, my wife was despondent and my editor enraged. To them, it was plain to see I needed something, anything, and fast.

Unbeknownst to me, my wife immediately wrote a letter to my doctor, pleading with him to put me on medication. Midway through my second session, I must have convinced him as well because he reached into a drawer and pulled out some samples of a drug called Cymbalta.

He said it could take a few weeks to kick in. Best case, he said, would be four days. He also said that its reaction time would depend on how much body fat I had; the more I had, the longer it would take. That was a good sign for me. By August, far from putting on the Katrina 15, I had become a skeletal version of my pre-K self.

And before I left that second session, he told me to change the message on my phone, that "emotionally unavailable" thing. Not funny, he said.

I began taking Cymbalta on Aug. 24 [2006] a Thursday. With practically no body fat to speak of, the drug kicked in immediately. That whole weekend, I felt like

I was in the throes of a drug rush. Mildly euphoric, but also leery of what was happening inside of me. I felt off balance. But I felt better, too.

I told my wife this but she was guarded. I've always heard that everyone else notices changes in a person who takes an anti-depressant before the patient does, but that was not the case with me.

"I feel better," I told Kelly but my long-standing gloom had cast such a pall over our relationship that she took a wait-and-see attitude.

By Monday, I was settled in. The dark curtain had lifted almost entirely. The despondency and incapacitation vanished, just like that, and I was who I used to be: energetic, sarcastic, playful, affectionate and alive.

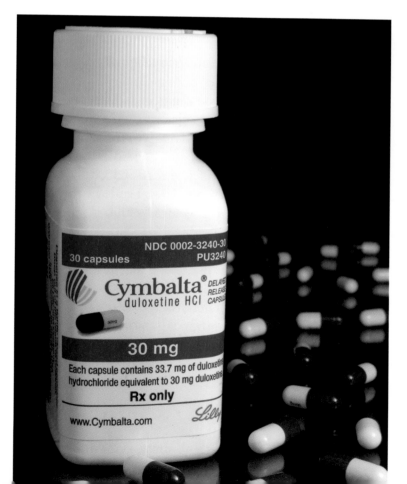

The viewpoint's author says that the drug Cymbalta, combined with psychological therapy and spousal support, helped him overcome his depression. (JB Reed/Bloomberg News/Landov)

I started talking to Kelly about plans—a word lacking from my vocabulary for months. Plans for the kids at school, extracurricular activities, weekend vacations. I had not realized until that moment that while stuck in my malaise, I had had no vision of the future whatsoever.

I wasn't planning anything. It was almost like not living.

Kelly came around to believing. We became husband and wife again. We became friends.

It all felt like a Come to Jesus experience. It felt like a miracle. But it was just medicine, plain and simple.

. . . .

I asked my doctor to tell me exactly what was wrong with me so I could explain it in this story. I will be candid and tell you I still don't really understand it, the science of depression, the actions of synapses, transmitters, blockers and stimulants.

I've never been much at science. I guess I'm just a fragile poet after all.

The diagnoses and treatments for depression and anxiety are still a developing science. The *Diagnostic and Statistical Manual of Mental Disorders*—psychiatry's chief handbook—practically doubles in size every time it's reprinted, filled with newer and clearer clinical trials, research and explanations.

Does that mean more people are getting depressed? Or that science is just compiling more data? I don't know.

Measuring depression is not like measuring blood sugar. You don't hit a specified danger level on a test and then you're pronounced depressed. It is nuance and interpretation and there is still a lot of guesswork involved.

But here's my doctor's take: The amount of cortisol in my brain increased to dangerous levels. The overproduction, in turn, was blocking the transmission of serotonin and norepinephrine.

Some definitions: Cortisol is the hormone produced in response to chronic stress. Serotonin and norepinephrine are neurotransmitters—chemical messengers—that mediate messages between nerves in the brain, and this communication system is the basic source of all mood and behavior.

The chemistry department at the University of Bristol in England has a massive Web database for serotonin, titled, appropriately: "The Molecule of Happiness."

And I wasn't getting enough. My brain was literally shorting out. The cells were not properly communicating. Chemical imbalances, likely caused by increased stress hormones—cortisol, to be precise—were dogging the work of my neurotransmitters, my electrical wiring. A real and true physiological deterioration had begun.

I had a disease.

This I was willing to accept. Grudgingly, for it ran against my lifelong philosophy of self-determination.

I pressed my doctor: What is the difference between sad and depressed? How do you know when you've crossed over?

"Post-traumatic stress disorder is bandied about as a common diagnosis in this community, but I think that's probably not the case," he told me. "What people are suffering from here is what I call Katrina Syndrome—marked by sleep disturbance, recent memory impairment and increased irritability.

"Much of this is totally normal. Sadness is normal. The people around here who are bouncing around and giddy, saying that everything is all right—they have more of a mental illness than someone who says, 'I'm pretty washed out.'

"But when you have the thousand-yard stare, when your ability to function is impaired, then you have gone from 'discomfort' to 'pathologic.' If you don't feel like you can go anywhere or do anything—or sometimes, even more—then you are sick."

And that was me.

And if that is you, let me offer some unsolicited advice, something that you've already been told a thousand times by people who love you, something you really ought to consider listening to this time: Get help.

. . . .

I hate being dependent on a drug. Hate it more than I can say. But if the alternative is a proud stoicism in the face of sorrow accompanied by prolonged and unspeakable despair—well, I'll take dependency.

I can live with it. I can live with anything, I guess. For now.

Cymbalta is a new generation of anti-depressant, a combination of both selective serotonin and norepinephrine re-uptake inhibitors—SSRIs and SNRIs—the two common drugs for anxiety and depression.

I asked my doctor why he selected it over, say, Prozac or Wellbutrin or any of the myriad anti-depressants whose brand names have become as familiar as aspirin in our community.

He replied: "It's a roll of the dice." He listened to my story, observed me and made an educated guess. If it didn't work, he said, we'd try something else.

But it worked.

Today, I can bring my kids to school in the morning and mingle effortlessly with the other parents.

Crowds don't freak me out. I'm not tired all day, every day. I love going to the grocery store. I can pump gas. I notice the smell of night-blooming jasmine and I play with my kids and I clean up after my dog and the simplest things, man—how had they ever gotten so hard?

The only effect I have noticed on my writing is that the darkness lifted. I can still channel anger, humor and irony—the three speeds I need on my editorial stick shift.

And I'm not the only one who senses the change. Everyone tells me they can see the difference, even readers. I'm not gaunt. I make eye contact. I can talk about the weather, the Saints, whatever; it doesn't have to be so dire, every word and motion.

Strange thing is this: I never cry anymore. Ever.

I tell you truthfully that I cried every day from Aug. 29 last year until Aug. 24 this year, 360 days straight. And then I stopped. I guess the extremes of emotion have been smoothed over but, truthfully, I have shed enough tears for two lifetimes.

Even at the Saints' "Monday Night Football" game, a moment that weeks earlier would have sent me reeling into spasms of open weeping, I held it together. A lump in my throat, to be sure, but no prostration anymore.

The warning labels on anti-depressants are loaded with ominous portent, everything from nausea to sexual dysfunction and, without going into more detail than I have already poured out here, let's just say that I'm doing quite well, thank you.

It's my movie now. I am part of the flow of humanity that clogs our streets and sidewalks, taking part in and being part of the community and its growth. I have clarity and oh, what a vision it is.

But I am not cured, not by any means. Clinical trials show Cymbalta has a 80-percent success rate after six months and I'm just two months in. I felt a backwards tilt recently—the long stare, the pacing, it crept in one weekend—and it scared me so badly that I went to the doctor and we agreed immediately to increase the strength of my medication.

Before Katrina, I would have called somebody like me a wuss. Not to my face. But it's what I would have thought, this talk of mood swings and loss of control, all this psychobabble and hope-dope.

What a load of crap. Get a grip, I would have said.

And that's exactly what I did, through a door that was hidden from me, but that I was finally able to see.

I have a disease. Medicine saved me. I am living proof.

Emphasis on living.

GLOSSARY

amygdala An almond-shaped structure in the temporal lobe of the brain and a part of the limbic system. It is involved in the processing of emotions and memories and is implicated in many psychiatric disorders.

antidepressant A medication used to treat depression. Drug groups known as SSRIs (selective serotonin reuptake inhibitors), MAOIs (monoamine oxidase inhibitors) and tricyclics are particularly associated with the term.

atypical depression A subtype of major depression that differs from melancholic depression in that patients react positively to external events, plus they experience two or more of the following symptoms: Significant weight gain (as opposed to weight loss), hypersomnia (as opposed to insomnia), leaden paralysis, and sensitivity to personal rejection.

bipolar disorder A depressive disorder in which a person alternates between episodes of major depression and mania.

catatonic depression A rare subtype of major depression characterized by at least two of the following symptoms: Stupor, excessive motor activity, extreme negativism, peculiarities in voluntary movement, and repetition of other people's words or actions.

clinical trials Trials to evaluate the effectiveness and safety of medications or medical devices by monitoring their effects on large groups of people.

depression A mood disorder characterized by a range of symptoms that may include feeling down most of the time, loss of pleasure, feelings of worthlessness, and suicidal thoughts, as well as physical states that may affect eating and sleeping and other activities.

depressive disorder	A group of diseases including major depressive disorder (commonly referred to as major depression), dysthymia, bipolar disorder (manic depression), postpartum depression, and seasonal affective disorder.
Diagnostic and Statistical Manual of Mental Disorders, 4th Edition (DSM-IV)	A book published by the American Psychiatric Association that gives general descriptions and characteristic symptoms of different mental illnesses. Physicians and other mental health professionals use the *DSM-IV* to confirm diagnoses for mental illnesses. The next edition of the *DSM* is scheduled for 2011.
dopamine	A neurotransmitter known to have multiple functions depending on where it acts. Dopamine is thought to regulate emotional responses and play a role in schizophrenia and cocaine abuse.
dysthymia	A type of depressive disorder that is less severe than major depressive disorder but is more persistent. The *DSM-IV* mandates the same symptoms as for major depression, except for suicidality, but requires only three symptoms in all, so long as they have persisted over two years.
electroconvulsive therapy (ECT)	A treatment for severe depression that involves passing a low-voltage electric current through the brain. The person is under anesthesia at the time of treatment. ECT is not commonly used in children and adolescents.
electroencephalography(EEG)	A method of recording the electrical activity in the brain through electrodes attached to the scalp.
hippocampus	A seahorse-shaped structure located within the brain considered an important part of the limbic system. It functions in learning, memory, and emotion.
limbic system	A group of brain structures—including the amygdala, hippocampus, septum, and basal ganglia—that works to help regulate emotion, memory, and certain aspects of movement.
major depressive disorder	Major depression, also known as clinical depression or unipolar depression, is a type of depressive disorder characterized by a long-lasting depressed mood or marked loss of interest or pleasure in nearly all activities. The *DSM-IV* lists nine symptoms for

major depression, five or more of which must be present over the same two-week period, including one of the following: 1) feeling depressed most of the day, nearly every day, or 2) experiencing markedly diminished pleasure. There are several different subtypes of major depression.

mania   Feelings of intense mental and physical hyperactivity, elevated mood, and agitation.

manic depression   *See* bipolar disorder.

melancholic depression   A subtype of major depression with an emphasis on lack of pleasure or lack of reactivity to pleasure. Other characteristics include (three or more): depressed mood, depression at worst in the morning, early-morning awakening, psychomotor agitation or retardation, significant weight loss, and inappropriate guilt.

monoamine neurotransmitter   A group of neurotransmitters derived from certain kinds of amino acids. Monoamine neurotransmitters include dopamine, norepinephrine, and serotonin.

monoamine oxidase inhibitors (MAOIs)   A type of antidepressant that works by blocking monoamine oxidase, an enzyme that degrades monoamine neurotransmitters.

neurons (nerve cells)   Specialized cells that carry "messages" through an electrochemical process that uses electrical signals and chemical substances called neurotransmitters.

neurotransmitters   Chemical substances that transmit information between neurons. Neurotransmitters are released by neurons into the extracellular space at synapses. There are several different neurotransmitters, including acetylcholine, dopamine, gamma aminobutyric acid (GABA), norepinephrine, and serotonin.

norepinephrine   Also called noradrenaline, it is a monamine neurotransmitter, produced both in the brain and in the peripheral nervous system. It seems to be involved in arousal, reward, regulation of sleep and mood, and the regulation of blood pressure.

placebo (sugar pill)	A technique or medication that contains no active ingredient and presumably therefore has no physical benefit. Placebos are generally administered in such a way that the recipients believe they are receiving the active treatment.
postpartum depression	A type of depressive disorder that occurs in women within four weeks of childbirth. Most new mothers suffer from some form of the "baby blues." Postpartum depression, by contrast, is major depression, thought to be triggered by changes in hormonal flows associated with childbirth.
premenstrual syndrome	A variety of physical and psychological symptoms sometimes preceding the monthly onset of menstruation and ending when menstruation begins.
psychiatrist	A medical doctor (MD) who specializes in treating mental diseases. A psychiatrist evaluates a person's mental and physical health and can prescribe medications.
psychoanalysis	A therapeutic method, originated by Sigmund Freud, for treating mental disorders by investigating the interaction of conscious and unconscious elements in the patient's mind and bringing repressed fears and conflicts into the conscious mind, using techniques such as dream interpretation and free association.
psychologist	A mental health professional who has received specialized training in the study of the mind and emotions. A psychologist usually has an advanced degree such as a doctor of philosophy (PhD).
psychotherapy	A treatment method for mental illness in which a patient discusses his or her problems and feelings with a psychiatrist, psychologist, or counselor. Psychotherapy can help individuals change their thought or behavior patterns or understand how past experiences affect current behaviors.
psychotic depression	A rare subtype of major depression characterized by delusions or hallucinations such as believing you are someone you are not and hearing voices.

schizophrenia   A chronic, severe, and disabling brain disease. People with schizophrenia often suffer terrifying symptoms such as hearing internal voices or believing that other people are reading their minds, controlling their thoughts, or plotting to harm them. These symptoms may leave them fearful and withdrawn. Their speech and behavior can be so disorganized that they may be incomprehensible or frightening to others.

seasonal affective disorder (SAD)   A depressive disorder that appears in the fall or winter and goes away in spring, thought to be caused by lack of sunlight.

selective serotonin reuptake inhibitors (SSRIs)   A group of antidepressants that work by preventing the reuptake of the neurotransmitter serotonin, thus maintaining higher levels of serotonin in the brain.

serotonin   A monoamine neurotransmitter that regulates many functions, including mood, appetite, and sensory perception.

STAR*D   Sequenced Treatment Alternatives to Relieve Depression (STAR*D), the largest and longest study done to evaluate the effectiveness of different antidepressant treatments.

synapse   The site where neurons communicate with each other.

tricyclics   The oldest group of antidepressants. Tricyclics work by blocking the reuptake of several different neurotransmitters, including serotonin and norepinephrine.

CHRONOLOGY

ca. 460 BC– AD 200	The ancient Greek theory of the four humors, ascribed to Hippocrates (460–370 BC) and extended by Galen (AD 131–200), holds that melancholia is caused by too much black bile.
ca. 900	Muslim psychologist Ishaq ibn Imran's essay "Maqala fi-l-malikhuliya" refers to a mood disorder known as "malikhuliya," which means "melancholia."
	The book *Leechdom, Wortcunning and Star Craft of Early England* gives herbal remedies for melancholia as well as for hallucinations, mental vacancy, dementia, and folly.
ca. 1020	Persian physician Avicenna's *The Canon of Medicine* describes a number of neuropsychiatric conditions, including melancholia.
1564	Giulio Cesare Aranzi (aka Julius Caesar Arantius) names a region of the brain the "hippocampus."
1621	Robert Burton publishes *The Anatomy of Melancholy*.
1695	Humphrey Ridley publishes *The Anatomy of the Brain*.
1755	J.B. Le Roy uses electroconvulsive therapy [ECT] for mental illness.

1812   Benjamin Rush writes the first American book on psychiatry, *Medical Inquiries and Observations upon the Diseases of the Mind.*

1849   British psychiatrist John Charles Bucknill uses electrical stimulation of the skin and potassium oxide to treat asylum patients with melancholic depression.

1860   Karl L. Kahlbaum describes and names "catatonia."

1880   Seven categories of mental illness are used for U.S. census data: mania, melancholia, monomania, paresis, dementia, dipsomania, epilepsy.

ca. 1883   German psychiatrist Emil Kraepelin writes *Compendium der Psychiatrie,* in which he first presents a classification of mental disorders. Kraepelin made an important differentiation between manic-depressive psychosis (bipolar disorder) and schizophrenia.

1891   Wilhelm von Waldeyer coins the term *neuron.*

1897   Charles Scott Sherrington coins the term *synapse.*

1903   British neurologist Thomas R. Elliott proposes the concept of chemical neurotransmitters.

1909   Clifford Beers founds the organization currently named Mental Health America.

1917   Sigmund Freud publishes *Mourning and Melancholia.*

1938   Ugo Cerletti and Lucino Bini treat human patients with electroshock therapy.

1940 Vittorio Erspamer isolates serotonin from rabbit tissue and names it *enteramine.*

1946 Ulf von Euler identifies norepinephrine (noradrenaline) in extracts of adrenergic nerves from different species.

1948 Maurice M. Rapport, Arda Green, and Irvine Page isolate serotonin from blood serum.

1949 Australian psychiatrist John Cade introduces the use of lithium to treat psychosis.

1951 The first modern antidepressant, called iproniazid, is discovered while doctors are studying tuberculosis medications. Iproniazid is a monoamine oxidase inhibitor (MAOI).

1952 The first edition of the *Diagnostic and Statistical Manual of Mental Disorders* (*DSM-I*) is published by the American Psychiatric Association.

1953 Betty Twarog and Irvine Page identify serotonin in the brain.

1956 Roland Kuhn discovers the antidepressant effects of imipramine, a tricyclic antidepressant.

1957 Arvid Carlsson demonstrates that dopamine is a brain neurotransmitter.

1960 Psychiatrist Thomas Szasz publishes *The Myth of Mental Illness,* in which he says there is no such thing as mental illness.

1970s	Researchers at Eli Lilly, including Ray Fuller, Bryan Molloy, and David Wong, begin studying selective serotonin reuptake inhibitors (SSRIs). Their work leads to the discovery of Prozac.
1980	The American Psychiatric Association publishes the *DSM-III*.
1987	Prozac is approved for use by the U.S. Food and Drug Administration (FDA).
1994	The American Psychiatric Association publishes the *DSM-IV*.
2001	Eli Lilly's patent on Prozac expires.
2004	The FDA orders pharmaceutical companies to put "black box" warnings on the labels of antidepressants to advise consumers that the medications could cause suicidal tendencies in individuals younger than age eighteen.
2006	The FDA extends the black box warnings to young adults aged eighteen to twenty-four.

ORGANIZATIONS TO CONTACT

Alliance for Human Research Protection (AHRP)
142 West End Ave.,
Ste. 28P
New York, NY 10023
www.ahrp.org

The AHRP is a national network of laypeople and professionals dedicated to advancing responsible and ethical medical research practices and exposing corruption in the field of health care. The group speaks out against the widespread prescribing of antidepressants and other drugs. It publishes an online info-mail containing news articles about medical fraud and corruption.

American Foundation for Suicide Prevention (AFSP)
120 Wall St.,
22nd Fl.
New York, NY 10005
(888) 333-2377
fax: (212) 363-6237
www.afsp.org

The AFSP is a nonprofit organization dedicated to reducing loss of life from suicide. The AFSP works to prevent suicides and reach out and assist those who have been affected by suicide. The organization sponsors local "Out of the Darkness Over-night Walks" to bring together people who have been touched by suicide and to raise awareness about suicide prevention. AFSP's quarterly newsletter *Lifesavers* helps the AFSP to communicate and disseminate information about depression and suicide prevention to the public.

American Psychiatric Association (APA)
1000 Wilson Blvd.,
Ste. 1825
Arlington, VA
22209-3901
(888) 357-7924
www.psych.org

The APA is an organization of professionals working in the field of psychiatry. The APA works to advance the profession and promote the highest quality care for individuals with mental illnesses and their families. Additionally, the APA educates the public about mental health, psychiatry, and successful treatment options. The organization publishes a twice-monthly newsletter, *Psychiatric News*, as well as several journals including the *American Journal of Psychiatry* and *Psychiatric Services*.

Depression and Bipolar Support Alliance (DBSA)
730 N. Franklin St., Ste. 501
Chicago, Il 60610-7224
(800) 826 -3632
fax: (312) 642-7243
www.dbsalliance.org

The DBSA is a leading patient-directed national organization focusing on depression and bipolar disease, the two most prevalent mental illnesses. The organization provides up-to-date information about mental illness, holds an annual depression and bipolar conference, supports mental health research, and sponsors hundreds of grassroots support groups across the country. DBSA publishes more than two dozen educational materials about living with mood disorders. In addition to the main DBSA Web site, the organization provides information tailored to specific concerns in the following affiliated Web sites: www.rebeccasdream.org, www.sleeplessinamerica.org, www.peersupport.org, www.peershelpingpeers.org, and www.facingus.org.

International Foundation for Research and Education on Depression (iFred)
2017-D Renard Ct.
Annapolis, MD 21401
(410) 268-0044
fax: (443) 782-0739
www.ifred.org

The iFred is a nonprofit organization dedicated to researching the causes of depression, supporting those dealing with depression, and combating the stigma associated with depression. iFred offers downloadable brochures and flyers on its Web site.

Mental Health America
2000 N. Beauregard St., 6th Fl.
Alexandria, VA 22311
(703) 684-7722
fax: (703) 684-5968
www.mentalhealthamerica.net

Mental Health America (formerly known as the National Mental Health Association) is a nonprofit organization dedicated to helping all people live mentally healthy lives. The organization educates the public about ways to preserve and strengthen mental health; fights for access to effective mental health care; fights to end discrimination against people with mental and addictive disorders; and fosters innovative mental health research, treatment, and support services. Mental Health America issues several e-mail newsletters, such as the *Bell*, and produces several fact sheets and informational documents.

National Alliance on Mental Illness (NAMI)
2107 Wilson Blvd., Ste. 300
Arlington, VA 22201-3042
(703) 524-7600
fax: (703) 524-9094
www.nami.org

The NAMI is a national grassroots mental health organization that seeks to eradicate mental illness and improve the lives of persons with serious mental illness and their families. NAMI works through advocacy, research, education, and support. The organization publishes a periodic magazine called the *Advocate*.

National Institute of Mental Health (NIMH)
Science Writing, Press, and Dissemination Branch
6001 Executive Blvd., Rm. 8184, MSC 9663
Bethesda, MD 20892-9663
(866) 615-6464
fax: (301) 443-4279
www.nimh.nih.gov

The NIMH is the leading agency of the U.S. government concerned with mental health issues. The mission of NIMH is to reduce the burden of mental illness and behavioral disorders through research on mind, brain, and behavior. The NIMH publishes various booklets, fact sheets, and easy-to-read materials on mental health issues.

Postpartum Support International (PSI)
PO Box 60931
Santa Barbara, CA 93160
(805) 967-7636
fax: (323) 204-0635
www.postpartum.net

PSI is a nonprofit organization whose mission is to promote awareness of pregnancy-related mood disorders and to advocate, educate, and provide support for maternal mental health worldwide. The organization works at the grassroots level to support, educate, and advocate for people living with mental illness through various activities. PSI publishes the *PSI News* which provides up-to-date information on conferences, resources, research, and PSI events.

Screening for Mental Health, Inc. (SMH)
One Washington St., Ste. 304
Wellesley Hills, MA 02481
(781) 239-0071
fax: (781) 431-7447
www.mentalhealth screening.org

SMH is a nonprofit organization that develops and administers large-scale mental health screenings, such as the SOS Signs of Suicide High School Program and National Depression Screening Day. The organization seeks to identify people with mental illness and help them to seek treatment. The organization produces fact sheets and other educational materials about suicide, alcoholism, and depression.

Society for Neuroscience (SFN)
1121 Fourteenth St. NW, Ste. 1010
Washington, DC 20005
(202) 962-4000
fax: (202) 962-4941
www.sfn.org

The SFN works to provide professional development activities and educational resources for neuroscientists and to educate the public about the findings, applications, and potential of neuroscience research. The organization has several online publications, including *Brain Research Success Stories* and *Brain Briefings*, periodic newsletters explaining how basic neuroscience discoveries lead to clinical applications.

Substance Abuse and Mental Health Services Administration (SAMHSA)
Center for Mental Health Services
1 Choke Cherry Rd., Rockville, MD 20857
(240) 276-1310
fax: (240) 276-1320
www.samhsa.gov

SAMHSA, part of the U.S. Department of Health and Human Services, seeks to ensure that people who suffer from mental health or substance abuse disorders have the opportunity to live fulfilling and meaningful lives as expressed in the agency's mission statement, "A Life in the Community for Everyone." SAMHSA works to expand and enhance prevention and early intervention programs and improve the quality, availability, and range of mental health and substance abuse treatment and support services in local communities across the United States. The agency publishes the bimonthly newsletter *SAMSHA News* as well as various recurring statistical reports on mental health and substance abuse.

FOR FURTHER READING

Books

Ronald W. Dworkin, *Artificial Happiness: The Dark Side of the New Happy Class.* New York: Carroll & Graf, 2006.

Angus Gellatly, *Introducing Mind and Brain: A Graphic Guide to the Science of Your Grey Matter.* Cambridge, UK: Totem, 2008.

Jonathan Haidt, *The Happiness Hypothesis.* New York: Basic Books, 2006.

Nicholas Heiney, *The Silence at the Song's End.* Edited by Libby Purves and Duncan Wu Westleton. Suffolk, UK: Songsend, 2007.

Allan V. Horwitz and Jerome C. Wakefield, *The Loss of Sadness: How Psychiatry Transformed Normal Sorrow into Depressive Disorder.* New York: Oxford University Press USA, 2007.

Peter D. Kramer, *Against Depression.* New York: Penguin, 2006.

Darian Leader, *The New Black: Mourning, Melancholia and Depression.* New York: Penguin, 2008.

Bruce E. Levine, *Surviving America's Depression Epidemic: How to Find Morale, Energy, and Community in a World Gone Crazy.* White River Junction, VT: Chelsea Green, 2007.

Kate Scowen, *My Kind of Sad: What It's Like to Be Young and Depressed.* New York: Annick, 2006.

Gordon Smith, *Remembering Garrett: One Family's Battle with a Child's Depression.* New York: Carroll & Graf, 2006.

Vatsal Thakkar, *Depression and Bipolar Disorder.* New York: Chelsea House, 2006.

J. Mark G. Williams, John D. Teasdale, Zindel V. Segal, and Jon Kabat-Zinn, *The Mindful Way Through Depression: Freeing Yourself from Chronic Unhappiness.* New York: Guilford, 2007.

Terrie Williams, *Black Pain: It Just Looks like We're Not Hurting.* New York: Scribner, 2008.

PERSPECTIVES ON DISEASES AND DISORDERS

Periodicals

Charles Barber, "The Medicated Americans: Antidepressant Prescriptions on the Rise," *Scientific American*, February 2008.

Sharon Begley, "Happiness: Enough Already," *Newsweek*, February 2, 2008.

R.H. Belmaker and Galila Agam, "Major Depressive Disorder," *New England Journal of Medicine*, January 3, 2008.

Angela Bischoff, "Sounding the Pharma Alarm: Four Accounts of the Rise of the Pharmaceutical Industry," *Briarpatch*, September/October, 2007.

B. Bower, "Dangerous DNA: Genes Linked to Suicidal Thoughts with Med Use," *Science News*, October 6, 2007.

Peter W. Crownfield, "Depressing News About Antidepressants: What Parents Need to Know," *To Your Health*, October 2007.

David Dobbs, "A Depression Switch?" *New York Time*, April 2, 2006.

Economist, "Hope from a Pill: Antidepressants," March 1, 2008.

Ann Garvin and Christopher Damson, "The Effects of Idealized Fitness Images on Anxiety, Depression and Global Mood States in College Age Males and Females," *Journal of Health Psychology*, 2008.

Jeffrey Kluger, "When Worry Hijacks the Brain," *Time*, August 13, 2007.

Susan J. Landers, "Fears About Antidepressants Are Causing Many People Not to Take Antidepressants," *American Medical News*, January 22, 2007.

Diana Mahoney, "Prozac No Better than Placebo in Teens with Substance Abuse Issues," *Family Practice News*, March 1, 2008.

John R. Pettinato, "Green-Eyed and Depressed: What's the Connection Between Mental Illness and Cornea Color?" *Discover*, June, 2003.

Evelyn Pringle, "Weighing Benefits of SSRIs Against Suicide Risk," *Lawyers and Settlements*, December 8, 2006.

Tina Hesman Saey, "Growing Up to Prozac: Drug Makes New Neurons Mature Faster," *Science News*, February 9, 2008.

Andrew Solomon, "Our Great Depression," *New York Times*, November 17, 2006.

Rob Stein and Marc Kaufman, "Depression Drugs Safe, Beneficial, Studies Say Suicide Risk Rejected, but Critics Question Validity of Findings," *Washington Post*, January 1, 2006.

Video

Depression and Bipolar Support Alliance, *The State of Depression in America*. Hosted by Mike Wallace. Indianapolis: Creative Street Media Group, 2006.

INDEX

A

Aberle, John, 63

Addis, Michael, 56, 60–61

Adjustment disorder, 19

Adolescent(s)
  girls, 65–66
  risk of suicide among, 22
  school health screening for, 9–14

African American women, 68–69

Against Depression (Kramer), 79, 80

Alliance for Human Research Protection (AHRP), 12, 13

American Psychiatric Association
  (APA), 27, 81
  on electroconvulsive therapy, 39, 104

Antidepressants
  are overprescribed, 92–98
  benefits of, 131–146
  focus on brain communication,
    47–48
  may be underprescribed, 83–91
  numbers prescribed, 93
  research for new types of, 37–39
  types of, 21–23, 36–37

Anxious depression, 30–31

Aronson, Phil, 61–62

Atypical depression, 28–30

B

Bereavement, 94–95, 96

Bipolar disorder, 18, 28, 34
  as hidden disability, 113–120
  rapid cycling, 65

Braff, Zach, 63

Brain-derived neurotrophic factor
  (BDNF), 38

Breggin, Peter, 105

Brody, Jane, 99

Burguieres, Philip, 62–63

Bush, George W., 10

C

Carmichael, Mary, 55

Carpenter, Linda L., 32

Cavett, Dick, 100

Children
  anxious depression in, 31
  dysthymic disorder in, 21